The Claw Of The Magnolia

Pedram Navab

SPUYTEN DUYVIL
New York City

This book is a work of fiction. Names, characters, places, and incidents either are products of the author's imagination or are used fictitiously. Any resemblance to actual events or locales or persons, living or dead, is entirely coincidental or has been altered.

© 2022 Pedram Navab
ISBN 978-1-956005-54-7

Library of Congress Cataloging-in-Publication Data

Names: Navab, Pedram, author.
Title: The claw of the magnolia / Pedram Navab.
Description: New York City : Spuyten Duyvil, [2022]
Identifiers: LCCN 2022027711 | ISBN 9781956005547 (paperback)
Subjects: LCGFT: Detective and mystery fiction. | Novels.
Classification: LCC PS3614.A926 C53 2022 | DDC 813/.6--dc23/eng/20220624
LC record available at https://lccn.loc.gov/2022027711

The often hazy line of demarcation between all of nature's twins—two human beings held apart and together by genetic and emotional forces, two memories held apart and together by those who share them, even two forms of writing, the deeply factual and lyrically beautiful—is impressively traced in Pedram Navab's stunner of a book. Equally at home in the medical and literary fields, this book is truly a singular vision, a haunting elegy for sisters lost in their own twinned ways, and is not to be missed. Beautifully rendered, this one will stay with you long after the last page turns.

David Rocklin,
author of *The Luminist* and *The Night Language*

An evocative and unsettling novel that unspools in fragments and multiple narratives as surreal as Edgar Alan Poe and as sobering as an Emergency Room at midnight (and vice versa), this is a wondrous puzzle of a book that'll shake your snowglobe.

Mark Haskell Smith, author of *Blown*

Suitably set in H. P. Lovecraft's hometown, *The Claw of the Magnolia* is more than a carefully-plotted tale of suspense. Inside its charnel houses, beyond the secrets shared by twins, the mysteries of practicing medicine and the rituals that circumscribe the observance of seemingly opposing religions, Pedram Navab's chilling novel is an investigation into the liminal space between memory and imagination. As the characters are plunged deeper into their pasts to find that elusive understanding of the present, they discover, as will readers, how delicate the boundaries are between angels and demons, escape and erasure, and mercy killing and murder.

Jane Rosenberg LaForge,
author of *Sisterhood of the Infamous*

The Claw of the Magnolia is both profound and wickedly entertaining, filled with mesmerizing doubles (including twin sisters), ghosts, monsters, and mysteries winding through worlds seen and unseen. You'll find yourself torn between wanting to rip through a plot that's twisty as a thriller and yearning to linger in its philosophical mazes.

Dawn Raffel, author of *The Strange Case of Dr. Couney*

Pedram Navab's *The Claw of the Magnolia* is a novel of intrigue that will affect a reader. It is a highly creative and devilishly plotted tale of fate, filial and sisterly love, impossible yearnings, suicides, and the space between life and death. The dance of surprises and secrets, the surreal angst, and the macabre underlining will unsettle the reader's consistency of tastes, values, and memories, bringing them to a Barthesian blissful crisis. In the words of Kafka, this book is like "an axe for the frozen sea within us." It is because of books like *The Claw of the Magnolia* that meaningful literature remains alive.

Jorge Armenteros,
author of *The Striped Tunic Trilogy* and *Touch That Which You Cannot Possess*

Far more than a medical mystery, *The Claw of the Magnolia* erupts as a gothic tale of ghosts and lost manuscripts, madness and disease, and a cast of distinctive characters linked across time and place. With a phantastic imagination tempered by fascinating research, author Pedram Navab once again creates a dizzying world of spiritual mist, physical matter, and psychological horror. Diabolically entertaining!

Debra Di Blasi, author of *Birth of Eros* and *Selling the Farm*

Pedram Navab's *The Claw of the Magnolia* compellingly fuses multiple genres of fiction (mystery, historical, supernatural, epistolary, diaristic, etc.) within a Nabokovian meta-fictive frame. Traversing time and space, engaging a host of ghosts, the novel brims with intertextual references (Plath, Benjamin, Lovecraft, Poe, Wilde, Stevenson, Sartre, Keats, Kant, Bergson, Highsmith, etc.), Navab deftly engaging philosophy, neuroscience, memory, history, desire, loss, and grief. In short, Navab's *The Claw of the Magnolia* is an elusive, allusive combination puzzle memento mori.

John Madera,
author of *Nervosities* and *Among the Dynamos*

The claw
Of the magnolia,
Drunk on its own scents,
Asks nothing of life.

Sylvia Plath

I died so I could haunt you.

Torquil Campbell

Note

The last manuscript of Nadia Sullivan, Professor of Behavioral Neuroscience at Brown University, was found in her home shortly after her suspicious death in 1970. It was anonymously offered to and posthumously retained by The John Hay Library as part of its special collections. Recently, a large portion of its pages was ripped out and stolen.

Millie Howard
Head Librarian

PART I
THURSTON & MORGAN
& VINCENT

1996 | PROVIDENCE, RHODE ISLAND
THURSTON KAFKA

Day ten. The Man was still here, reading, agitated almost. He was looking for something, something that he had perhaps lost. But this wasn't accurate either. It was as if he wanted to find something that someone else had lost, and that he hoped to greedily retrieve for himself. I was looking at him, marking his mannerisms. He would come into the John Hay Library on Prospect Street, opposite the Van Wickle Gates of Brown University. He was an enigma, and the mystery of this library suited him.

The Man kept scavenging the library's rare books and archives, and its special collections. Although his manner was frenetic, there was an order to it. He would go to the special collections, retrieve a manuscript, and then sit at one of the old, heavy wooden tables. The Man would then start reading. And after only a few minutes when he couldn't find what he was looking for, he would return to the collections and repeat the process. He would only take one manuscript at a time. This went on daily for hours, six perhaps. I would then observe his dejected, withered face when he would open the outmoded, heavy doors of the library and leave. The Man would return the next day, and the following.

I was a graduate student at Brown, working on my dissertation thesis on the psychoanalytic theory of ghosts and the double in Victorian literature. I was specifically looking at three major texts: Stevenson's *The Strange Case of*

Dr. Jekyll and Mr. Hyde, Wilde's *The Picture of Dorian Gray*, and Poe's *The Fall of the House of Usher*. I must admit, it was an ambitious project, but I relished this arduous process, which involved extensive reading, researching, and reworking of other secondary texts. This was my life then, and I couldn't be happier to be placed in this intellectual milieu. I wanted to absorb all of history, all the intricate connections between the authors, past and present. Like Walter Benjamin, I yearned to study the dust that permeated the relics of history. I was so ambitious, so passionate, so in love with learning. I wished this love of learning would also bleed into my life. Regretfully, it did not.

I imagined myself in this baroque era. Brown, and this library, seemed exceptionally suited to me. In the Hay Library, I felt connected to H.P. Lovecraft's collection of manuscripts and letters. I felt his spirit waft past me. I looked wondrously at the three books in this library that were bound in human skin and thought about their origins in blood, about the doctors who had access to cadavers and were commissioned to do this. I would also meticulously research the other collections at the Annmary Brown Memorial, where the body of Nicholas Brown's daughter, Annmary, was buried in an enclosure at the east end of the building. It seemed befitting me, this Gothic outpouring, Lovecraft's and Brown's ghosts hovering above me in the environs of the Hay. I wondered what other ghosts I would find in this lonely and strange space.

Yet, despite all the ghostly beginnings and haunted intimations at Brown, I thought about this Man. To me, he was like Sartre's Self-Taught Man. He exuded that Man's tenacity, strong will, and independence. He didn't need a thing from anyone. His answers lay in the books, and he would wrest these from them alone. That was his main objective, to find an answer to the puzzle. The Man was not concerned about anything else. He was self-sufficient. His actions and resourcefulness assured me of this. But unlike the Self-Taught Man who would try to learn all of history and life's wisdom, patiently and methodically, this Man wanted answers without hesitation. He was agitated. He was impatient. He was hungry. And that both bothered and fascinated me.

And then I knew that I recognized him not as the Self-Taught Man, but rather as Poe's Man of the Crowd. He really was the Man of the Crowd, in the not-so-crowded Hay. He was extremely thin and feeble, but so very relentless. His face had a peculiar idiosyncrasy, but it was really the hollowed and elongated features of it that made it so strange. His face was a rugged terrain. He had abnormally long and distorted limbs that made him look like a deformed monk, straight out of a Gothic novel. His spine was curved, and one could observe the slithering caterpillar in him when he walked. He towered above me at six and a half feet in height, possibly taller. Like Poe's Man, he was frenetically driven and would push himself doggedly into the heart of the mighty London if given the chance. Although he appeared thin and weak, with brittle bones, I could imagine that he would outmaneuver me through the bazaars and shops in London if we found ourselves there. I could see deep crime inscribed in him, and, like the unnamed narrator of Poe's tale, I was deeply and perversely fascinated by his narrative. I aimed to find out more about the Man. I would not rest until I did.

Dear Dead Sister,

I'm afraid these letters from Bay State Correctional Center find you too late. Ours was always a missed encounter, wasn't it? I was always too early. You were always too late. In our last days together, you didn't even have the fucking gall to show up. You were gone before you arrived. But what remained was always your scent. Christian Dior's *Poison*, the fragrance you bought at the Macy's in Warwick Mall. It was your signature scent. Everyone knew it. We could smell you so far away but never in a bad way. You didn't reek of fragrance, like those high school guys who tried to impress us with their Cavaricci pants and pungent *Drakkar Noir* colognes. Remember those losers? Instead, you made the perfume your own. You were Poison. Poison was you. You wore it like a skin-tight dress that makes you look flattering in all the right places. 36-24-36 inches. (You had the ideal hotness proportions, but you never knew that, did you?) I thought that poison would be the death of you. Instead, fire won out. But you know what? I smell you more powerfully now than when you were alive. Do you remember that time when we went to the Walgreens on Atwells Avenue? We were fifteen years old then and inseparable, as twins are, before we abruptly drifted apart. You had sprayed two pumps of the cheap drugstore perfume *Demeter Kitten Fur* because the name made you laugh. It was not the sort of perfume you'd wear. You were not cheap. Not in the least. Even then, you were considered regal. Everybody thought so, even if you didn't believe it yourself. You were never confident that way, although the kids at Mount Pleasant High thought you were a stuck-up, fucking bitch. "Your sister Mallory is such a stuck-up, fucking bitch," they would tell me. I don't know why I didn't defend you or even tell you that they called you such names. Perhaps jealousy? Perhaps because words don't really matter when people have already made up their minds? Maybe you already knew. But I knew better. You were way too self-conscious and shy. Even though we were identical twins, you had the looks. I was a cheap copy. But you never knew who you really were. I digress. More about that later. Back to the *Kitten*. The label beneath the perfume said the fragrance was inspired by the sweet smell behind a kitten's neck. We never had kittens, so how were we to know if the scent was authentic? But when you sprayed that on your skin, the aroma transformed into a powdery musk. You laughed, your teeth white and bright as Providence's first snow before the snow had a chance to change into icy filth over the next few months. (I almost loved that town when you were by my side. Almost.) Then you sarcastically remarked, "The only thing that's missing is the purr." I laughed, but you remained dead serious as if the kitten had died and its scent was being harvested for these perfumes. "It's a goddamn animal, Morgan," you said. "Imagine if it had actually died." I then knew that, at your core, you wanted to change things in society, take an ethical stance, even though you aspired to be a runway model. Not that the two were mutually exclusive, but still. Now, I only smell the scent of the *Demeter Kitten Fur* on you, not the *Poison,* although the *Kitten* was such a brief whiff on your skin. Do you know this is what we call olfactory memory? The sense of smell is more closely linked with memory than any of the other senses. The primary olfactory cortex of the brain and the hippocampus have connections with the amygdala. It is the amygdala, that almond-shaped cluster of nuclei, which is involved in the formation of memories of emotional experiences. The doctor in me comes out when I'm explaining these scientific terms to you. Forgive me. I don't mean to sound erudite. But, once again, I'm afraid that I'm too early and you're gone before you managed to arrive. Only the *Demeter Kitten Fur* remains as a hallucinatory odor. I still can't hear the purr.

xx,

Sister

The lush garden separates them, the garden with the oleander, hibiscus, and magnolia. It separates Vincent Duchene, recently diagnosed with lung cancer, and his neighbor, Nadia Sullivan, slowly succumbing to her own similar death. He rests in his cubular sitting room, the one with the Ottoman rug and the Grecian urn. These quarters will soon become his own private mausoleum as he slowly withers away. In the bedroom of her home on 1111 Angell Street, Nadia sits on her baroque bed. She looks listlessly ahead, thinking about more practical things: the hair on the bathroom floor; her empty, open shampoo bottle; the dirty mirror that she forgot to clean again, projecting the frantic skeleton that she has slowly become.

Through the open windows adjacent to one another, Vincent watches Nadia every day to see who will succumb first. But, perhaps, it's not that. Perhaps he looks to her to see if he's progressing as he should. Perhaps he looks to her for comfort, for a remote intimacy. Vincent reviews her patterns and stages. They are latent mirrors of one another, Vincent and Nadia. When she coughs blood more forcefully, he knows that in a month, the same fate will befall him. When he is febrile for an extended period, he knows that Nadia has already experienced that stage of illness. They were diagnosed with lung cancer exactly one month apart. Though he finds it odd, his symptoms resemble hers, separated by that duration. Nadia's pattern will emerge in him in such a cycle.

It is an unusually wet and frigid summer in Providence. The year is 1970. It is a chilly day, one that seems appropriate to the coldness that resides within them both. Sometimes the curtains are drawn; other days they're not. When the curtains are drawn open, he glimpses her scrawny body in the occasional sunlight. Frequently, the sunlight makes him uncomfortable, reminding him of brighter days past. Other times, the sunlight offers him hope of a future in which his cancer has remitted. On occasion, Nadia undresses before him. She demurely removes her short hijab and reveals her silk, paisley nightgown. Sometimes, she is completely naked, with her breasts and thick pubic hair on display. He's unsure whether she's conscious of his presence, of his panoptic gaze. She looks inwardly at her eroded body, at her eroded composition.

Vincent tries to examine Nadia's excavated chest, the bones jutting out. Her breasts are swollen, likely from the edema. The scar on her abdomen conjures up images of the jagged Pennine Alps in Switzerland, to where he had last traveled with his deceased wife. It was an uneventful marriage that had borne no children. Nadia has lost at least five kilograms since a fortnight ago. Her almost dark body resembles a lost continent, one that he's not afraid to traverse. He would like to caress her black nipples. He would like to run his fingers across her ever-expansive chest. He would like to measure the distance between her two engorged breasts. He would like to kiss her softly on the lips to gauge the degree of parched earth. He would like to do much more. He knows he can't. He is Europe. She is

Africa. The distance between them is too great. The great walls they've erected are too high. They remain as distant mirrors of one another.

On day eleven, I struck a conversation with the Man. He was selecting a manuscript on the psychological aspects of the Double. I realized that I had also glanced at this manuscript but had chosen not to give it an extensive read. The manuscript, which was written by Sara Michelson, dealt extensively with the Double's psychological underpinnings. The Man seemed absolutely rapt, as if this were the treasure that he had been looking for all these days, perhaps even years. This was probably not the best time to converse with him, but I did so anyway, thinking that the manuscript connected and bound us in some way.

As he was holding the manuscript, I started. *A thought-provoking manuscript, isn't it?* The Man looked at me, but his eyes were so fathomless that I could not capture his gaze. He was looking in my direction, but his glance was far off. It overlooked me. He replied. *Psychobiology, the interior of our minds, is the fabric of our identities. It makes us who we are. I don't think anyone would disagree with that notion.* Unlike his exaggerated and unkempt appearance, his manner of speaking was so refined and his tone so articulate, that I forgot this was the Man whom I had observed for the last two weeks. He had a slightly tinged English accent, but one that had been diluted over the years. I gathered that he must be an English transplant, who had somehow made his way to Providence. Maybe he had relatives or friends here. But despite my initial mistake in reading him, I highly doubted that he had anyone. His seclusion was an open book and was plainly written for others to read. He was a recluse. I was willing to wager a bet on this. *I detect an English accent,* I continued. *Do you have family here?* He again glanced at me, with his dysmorphic features, this time as if he were irritated with me and shocked that I would continue my questioning. His hollowed and vacuous eyes meant to say: *Don't you see that I'm trying to find some sort of treasure here? Now get on with your studies. I have work to do. At this moment, you are a complete pest to me.* But he said nothing and quickly looked away. *All right, then. I'll leave you alone. We'll talk again soon,* I remarked. The image of his blank and empty eyes would return. In them, I could see that he had brushed with Death, very gently, in another realm, but had returned to face his demons here on earth. I then returned to reading the manuscript. I ultimately left the Hay, disheartened and curious.

Excerpt | Sarah Michelson,
  "The Double as Aborted Fetus"

In *The Strange Case of Dr. Jekyll and Mr. Hyde*, Stevenson acutely portrays the discarded nature of man through the motif of Edward Hyde, who comes to resemble a troglodyte, an atavistic cannibal, an *id* to Jekyll's *ego*, engaging in evil to satisfy his own desires. Hyde must be "hid" precisely because this is the aspect of man that cannot be seen, that cannot be observed by a society mired in rules and laws. Hyde is the aborted fetus because the Law cannot reconcile him to society. Hyde is unencumbered by the Law. He has no use for it. He shuns it. He makes it evident that Law is a societal construct.

Every man has a Double, the aborted fetus. As Stevenson himself observes, there is a duality in man. Both evil and good occupy his nature, but the degree to which this becomes problematic is dependent on society's values and norms. In Stevenson's narrative, Jekyll severs his abominable and unimaginable acts and transfer these onto Hyde, who becomes the scapegoat and aborted fetus. What cannot be accomplished through Jekyll is relegated to Hyde to commit. The formation of this other identity, this Hyde, is essential for Jekyll to continue to survive. This cast-off is indispensable, insofar as it distances Jekyll from his own evil nature, his Hyde (Hide).[1*] But even though Jekyll is the epitome of British society, a respected physician, he carries this secret on himself, as it were. His name gives him away.

---

1 Nadia Sullivan, "Élan Vital: A Study in Life Unexplained." The John Hay Library, Brown University (1971)

(Je) Kyll, could perhaps be read as (I) Kill. A killer needs an aborted fetus to justify his killings.

Dearest Sister,

You never wanted to be one of the cool kids. I hated that about you. You were untouchable, too cool for school, always somewhere else but never here when I desperately needed you. It's as if you were born in a different time and place, as if you knew that you could never belong here, with us, with me. You were extraterrestrial. I hope you're happy where you are now. I really mean that. I absolutely fucking mean that. High school trivialities never phased you. I, on the other hand, cared about being part of the cool kids' club, although I made it seem like I didn't care a thing for it. My goth attire and makeup were a way to conceal that. I disguised myself to be someone I wasn't, but you showed us your authentic self, pure and unclassifiable. Others couldn't pin you down. An enigma. A Russian doll, with so many layers that no one could find you. Although we were identical twins, I always wished I were you. Copies aren't always the same, you know. Things get lost when copied. DNAs and RNAs are misread and mutated during transcription and translation. The TATA box can be decoded incorrectly. But here I am, again, trying to impress you with my scientific jargon. I know it's of no use. Even in death, you're way cooler than I am, with my technical ramblings and all. My most distinct memories of you are the ones where you were not really you. Like the time when I entered your room and you had donned a short, black wig.

Your gloriously blonde hair was pinned up and concealed underneath all that black. You had put a fuchsia lipstick on. Fake mascara and a severe black eyeliner followed. I had never seen you like this, so glaring and provocative. Someone or something had taken over you. "Mallory, what are you doing?" I almost shouted, dumbfounded but also scared. You had turned around and said, almost sullenly and sentimentally, "This is how I imagine our mother to look like if we ever found her or if we were to meet her." Mother was a word or a being we never knew. Mother. Who was she? Father always omitted the subject, but we had guessed that she had an unfortunate demise. But we were never sure, were we? Our hopes clung to the fact that we knew nothing about her. I think we never wanted to ask because we never wanted to know. We were almost certain of her death, but there was that minuscule chance that she was alive. We clung to that hope, like death clings to life once life begins. We wanted so much to believe that she was alive, so we never wished to confirm her death. I asked why you thought Mother would look like the way you depicted her. "I don't know," you replied. "It's just a feeling, you know. I tried to channel her. Don't you like it?" "So, you channeled a cabaret dancer?" I replied. "Don't be so cruel," you said. "I don't look like a dancer and neither did she." You had unintentionally veered into a terrain that was dangerous. With your past tense, you had pronounced her dead with one slip of a word. *Did.* You then realized this and remained silent. I remained in your room, anticipating your next response. "Here. Take a photo of me, Morgan," you haphazardly and unexpectedly requested, handing me the old Polaroid that dad had bought us at the Kmart that has since closed its doors. I accepted the camera. I took your photo. You were smiling, almost too forcefully, because you wanted the image of Mother to be a happy one. After a few minutes, the image miraculously developed. Even your Polaroid photo was beautiful. I don't know what happened to that image, but my memory of that episode is even stronger than the actual photo. Didn't Henri-Louis Bergson, the French philosopher, suggest that memory arises only if we don't experience the actual event? Perhaps, then, I never experienced you or the photo that day. Your image of you is latent, a little too late, just like you were. Always gone before you even arrived. You're always fucking gone, sister.

Lovingly,
Sister

VINCENT DUCHENE

Vincent gazes at Nadia every day. He glimpses a face of a skeleton. She has become so emaciated. Even when the curtains are closed, he surveys a shadow of a face that is slowly receding in size. She barely steps outside her room. In this space, she paces around so much. She resembles an enervated fly, buzzing around, knowing that death will soon come for it. Her movements are regularly erratic. She sleeps. She awakens. She walks. The pattern repeats itself. She sleeps. She awakens. She walks. And then she hesitates before moving again. She stops. She goes. She stops. She goes. Her eyes never look at the floor. She moves with pupils directed ahead. It's an exhausting game. Vincent, however, is fascinated. Nadia is a mouse trapped in a cage, but she doesn't want to escape. She desires capture. She desires to be caught by Death herself. She plays a game with Death. When one thinks Nadia has given up, she awakens and walks. Death hasn't captured her yet.

The flesh covering Nadia's jaw is eroding. Her mandible is becoming more distinct, exquisitely outlined, the closer Vincent looks at her. She will die elegantly, with her silk nightgown. She will be an exquisite corpse. Her skeleton will be more distinct than most. She will be cinematic. The thought comes to him and then slowly recedes. He feels ashamed for thinking so. Even now, he hasn't resorted to binoculars. He doesn't want to infringe upon her privacy to that extent. Sooner he will. He recognizes that.

Nadia's eyes are sharp, black, and proud. In them,

Vincent glimpses an image of his past. He has seen these eyes in a cadaver that he once dissected in medical school. They are the eyes of someone who has seen the past. They are eyes of someone who is not afraid to see the future death that will befall her. The eyes are disdainfully proud but also disdainfully sullen. If someone could just look at them and read them for Nadia, she would understand what she is feeling. But, other times, Nadia's eyes remind Vincent of a black cat. It was a cat that Vincent had seen as a child in his hometown of Stuttgart. It was a cat clamoring to eat a mouse that it had seen on the streets. The cat's eyes were hungry, not only for food but also for power. Hungry for so much power.

Vincent cannot speak with Nadia yet. Their continents are too far apart. Even when he thinks the gap will finally close, that the ice will melt and merge them closer, the glaciers shift. The glaciers drift them farther apart. The weather is much colder today. There is no sun to melt the ice. There is no sun to make the terrain more hospitable. There is no sun.

Nadia's curtains are closed more often now. He is confident that she still cannot see him. It's possible, though. After all, she closes her curtains more often now. She has grown more inward, drawn to herself, like Death itself who looks at Nadia more longingly. Her pain is seething through, boring her like a drill to wood. Her body, like infested wood, is slowly eroding. Vincent imagines himself as the parasitic worm that would gladly consume those termites for Nadia. If he could, he would extract and chew her black cancer, savoring every part until he spit it out.

Day fourteen was pivotal for the Man. He came to The Hay as soon as it opened its doors. His feverish energy was even more evident, and his eyes looked even wilder as if they had been lit by fire. He looked like a demon, agitated and mischievous. He walked briskly toward the section of psychobiological books, and, specifically, toward authors whose last names began with "S." There was no doubt that he was looking for Nadia Sullivan's manuscript, after having read Michelson's article. I was not familiar with Sullivan's work, but I recognized that she was a Professor Emeritus of Behavioral Neuroscience at Brown and had mysteriously died in 1970. The Man kept looking and seemed so frustrated. He was a fly, buzzing around the room, without a destination or aim. It was so sad to see. He was exploring every crevice in the library, although he was trying to conceal his actions. That's when I walked towards him and offered my assistance. *Can I help you find something? I know this library quite well. It's practically my home.* He looked at me, but somehow was not registering me. In fact, he was not looking at my eyes, but slightly above my head, and then mumbled: *Yes, please help me. I need all the help I can get. I don't know where to look.* It was an utter shock that he was even speaking to me, and, even more, that he was asking for my assistance. I quickly responded. *Of course! What are you looking for?* He was looking for his life, he said. He was looking for answers. He was looking for Nadia

Sullivan's last original manuscript, the one she wrote before she died. His first two responses were so cryptic that I had to convince myself that this was the same Man who wanted nothing to do with me, the same Man who refused to tell me anything about himself. And, now, here, in The Hay, he wanted me to help him find the key to his life. It was so unexpected. I used this exchange to ask him his name. He said that his name was not important, but that I should call him the Man because he really had no identity anyway, he had no name. *I don't know who I am anymore,* he muttered. *No matter,* I retorted. *Names are unnecessary anyway. My name is Thurston, if that makes a difference.* He looked at me again, with a dejected face and downcast gaze. *Please help me,* he implored again. *Please help me find Sullivan's manuscript.* He even showed me the citation in a recent article that he had read by Sara Michelson, the same article into which I had previously looked. The Man kept pointing to it, and literally pushing his finger into the article as if this physical force would somehow resurrect Sullivan's writing. *No, I understand. I'll help you find it.* We both kept looking for hours, and it was nowhere to be found. We even asked the reference librarian for help. She also saw a vacancy in the spot where Sullivan's monograph would be expected. Because the books at The Hay could not be checked out, the librarian thought it could perhaps be misplaced in another location. When the Man broached the topic of it being stolen, the librarian cringed as if this were blasphemy. *I think it's* misplaced, *Sir,* and she left it at that. Meanwhile, we looked some more and left when The Hay closed its doors at five, the sun still high in the summer sky.

Dear Mallory (or should I call you Char?),
I knew you had that tattoo—Char—etched on the outer edge of your left breast. But I know that you didn't think I knew. It was such an odd choice on the body. And Char? You hid the tattoo from me well, although you were not exactly meticulous. We never discussed where and how you got it. It was your secret, so I never pried. You had a right to your secrets. I had a right to mine. (You should know that a few years later after you got your tattoo, I also got one of a magnolia on my right inner thigh.) But I think of this word. Char. Was it short for Charlene or Charlotte? Is that who you wanted to be called? Was that the name of your lover? I know Mallory was not your favorite word. Mal, they called you. It's not a great name, I agree. "Mal" means evil in Spanish. I don't blame you. Char was much cooler. And you were cool. You deserved to be called Char. But seeing your burned face and body that night, I think about the ominous word that you left bare near your breast. Char means burnt. That name or nickname was an unfortunate choice, more than Mallory was. But let's get back to your presumed lover. We didn't talk about our sex lives much. Why was that? I guess because life was just more magical between us. We didn't need intrusion from a third party. We sufficed. We were enough. Without a mom, and only a father, we were self-sufficient. But I may have missed something. You had your tennis lessons in the spring and summer. Perhaps you

had met someone there. Like I said, I didn't pry. But no one dared talk to you in high school. You were considered exotic, untouchable in your detached, humble way. I don't imagine you could have been in a relationship. You were Mallory, the gorgeous sister, whom everyone wanted to emulate and fuck and hate and love, all at once. Perhaps I'm wrong. Maybe I didn't see something that I should've seen. Twins tend to overlook the most minute things. We don't always have good depth perception, don't you agree? We're not all telepathic, contrary to what everyone thinks. (Wasn't that the question we got asked the most when we were growing up?) Don't laugh. This is not the time for it. I'm putting the pieces of your death together. Slowly. I made an initial mistake in my assessment. I have had more time to think about things now. A lot of time. Maybe the fire wasn't your fault. Maybe this was the work of the South End Mafia who thought you were me, especially if you had worn that black wig. Your body dysmorphia and my bipolar disorder always complicate things. They lead us down an impossible terrain and insert themselves in places where they shouldn't be inserted. You know where I am now. In prison. I've gotten into trouble. But we'll talk about that later. All that I want to say to you now is that I'm sorry. I think that my actions may have unintentionally killed you. I'm not sure, though. Unfortunately, you may have been at the wrong place, at the wrong time. You were always too late. That was your flaw.

Regards,
Sister

Nadia is more difficult to look at. Her body, which was beautiful in its vulnerability, has now grown strange. It is unrecognizable. It has deformed into an uninviting landscape. Her breasts are sagging. Her belly has become edematous. The African continent that Vincent once recognized as beautiful has morphed into an extraplanetary enigma, one that he cannot explain. Occasionally, Vincent thinks that Nadia is sending him signals to touch her, to mold her body to a shape that he desires. But he cannot touch. He cannot mold. There is a mesosphere, perhaps a galaxy, separating him from her. There is no way he can reach her now, so vastly distanced she is from him. The pattern has shifted. He will no longer be following her bodily trajectory, at which he looked to gauge his own symptoms. He can clearly see that she is pregnant. Another being, another form, is residing within her. Vincent is even more intrigued. Will the child see the light of day? Or will it instead be snuffed like a candle that has just begun to burn? The plot of Nadia's story has changed. Vincent's narrative has undergone a change, too.

In her pregnancy, Nadia has become wilder. Her hair has greyed considerably since she began to show. It has also become wispier and drier. It resembles a dusty broom. Though he has difficulty discerning this in his binoculars, Nadia's pupils appear to have also grown more vibrant. They have grown more energetic. For the first time, he thinks she may be surveying *him*. He believes that he has also felt her hot, piercing pupils on him, a telescoping gaze that follows him. The submissive mouse has become the preying cat. Instinctively, he crouches from the window that has been his theater for the past months. He fears detection from a woman he has come to know as his unknowing confidante. *Does she, too, know that I'm withering away like she is?* Vincent ponders.

But the more important question that he is now forced to ask is how she became pregnant. No men reside in the house. Who could have impregnated her, he thinks? Within his subconscious, though, he knows the answer to the question that he asks. Intrigued, he continues to scrutinize Nadia, although more carefully now. She may be surveying him. He slowly recedes into the background. He recedes into the night, into the blackness of her body. There is a reason that windows have curtains.

To my utter shock and disappointment, I didn't see the Man the following day, or the day after that, or the next. His stint at The Hay had ended. He had disappeared for good, but he had piqued my curiosity even more, more than that day I had first met him. If he was looking for the key to his life, I was looking for the key that had somehow brought us together. His puzzle was my puzzle, too. If I didn't know where he had gone, I at least knew what he was searching for. It would be far too difficult to go inquiring about him. I was sure that he had no family in Providence. More importantly, I didn't know the Man's name. How could I find him? I was thus determined to seek that manuscript for which he was so rapturously hungry. I had put my graduate work on hold to look for this one item. How crazy it must seem! But my curiosity could not be quenched until I had read the mystery that lay in Nadia Sullivan's monograph. Why had the Man even been interested in psychobiology? He didn't seem the type. Were he and Nadia connected in some bizarre way? If this were so important to him, he surely would have exhausted all his opportunities to find this book. Something did not seem right. But I could not hope to get anywhere unless I found that monograph.

Mon cheri,

Élan vital: Vital force, in French. Do you remember when we both read Bergson's book *Creative Evolution* in AP French in our senior year in high school? It was as if an entire universe had opened for us. We "got" his concept of élan vital. An intuitive perception of experience and the flow of inner time. The paradoxical situation of humanity. The only species that wants to know the meaning of life is also the one who cannot do so. We must use our intuition, then, to place ourselves back within that vital force to overcome the obstacles of true knowledge. It sounds so much more complicated as I'm trying to explain it to you again. But something changed in us, resonated with us, when we read that book, as if the fact that we were twins meant something larger than us, larger than humanity. We were more than twins, more than sisters; we were part of a vital force that had meaning beyond itself. You became a philosophy major because of this work; I strayed to biology. The two disciplines were directly related to Bergson's work. But enough about him. No doubt, now, you know the meaning of life, and you can fathom the reason of your previous existence. You've left me in the dark to decipher this question by myself. I want to ask you whether our life had meaning, after all. I want to ask whether our absent mother was part of a vital equation in the scheme of things. I want to ask whether you're happy where you are.

Dead sister, I want to ask so many questions of you, but I don't know where you are anymore. I don't know where to fucking begin. The last time we saw one another was at Father's funeral. A black lace covered your face, but you still looked beautiful, like some tantalizing mosaic piece, a pattern of irregular pieces that are somehow connected to one another. Your face, scorched when I saw you on the hospital gurney, was something else. That's not the face that I see. Instead, I glimpse your previous diaphanous one, the one that shone the last time I saw you alive, as they were burying Father's coffin six feet underground, the sunlight hitting your face just so, when you become more heavenly and fragile. I thought you'd drift with him to the next world. You two were connected in a way that I never was. The last living image of you that I have is when you threw that sole rose, with your tears drenched in it, into his grave just as the sexton began to cover Father's coffin with dirt. It was classic cinema. (Maybe you were acting?) You wouldn't join him in the subterranean earth. Your fate would be different. You'd be burnt to smithereens. You'd be ashes.

Au revoir,
Morgan

Days pass. Though Nadia has become wilder, her languor projects through. With his binoculars, Vincent can see that the sockets of her eyeballs are conspicuously hollowed. The circles under her eyes are dark, grey. Her pupils are still feral. Nadia's eyelids suggest a droopiness that he hasn't seen before. There is no doubt about it. She is regressing to herself more forcefully. She is invading and attacking herself. *Can't she see this?* Vincent thinks. But he also discerns an uncontrolled energy that he has not sensed before. It's as if she can't cease and rest. She is continually moving more than she has before. Even at night, when he sometimes glimpses her shadow from the drawn lace curtains, she is still awake. She paces constantly in that small quarter of the room. *Why is she not sleeping?* he thinks. *Why is she not getting the rest she needs?* Perhaps it's the child that is growing within her. The child may be giving her unrest. But it's more than that, he thinks. There is unrest within her. Something more foreign than the cancer has invaded her body. She does not look as before. She is being attacked by all sides, not only from the tumor but from another malignancy that is far more dangerous, far more esoteric.

Momentarily, Vincent senses that Nadia may be asleep, although her eyes are widely open and vulnerable. It is how fish sleep, with their eyes open, he thinks. These fish that are deceptively awake, but dancing within the various stages of sleep. Nadia could be deceiving him, he believes. She could be surveying him even more closely. Vincent has made her life into a spectacle. She is giving him exactly what he desires. She is giving him life at its most skeletal, at its most basic. She is enacting bare life for him. Nadia is preparing him for his demise. She is his future mirror, his future narrative.

For three complete days, from nine a.m. when The Hay opened its doors, until five p.m., when it closed, I was looking for Sullivan's manuscript, the original compendium that only existed in this library. Due to the sheer volume of books, I couldn't look everywhere in the library. I had to figure a systematic way to approach this problem. How could I find a monograph that could be anywhere, or perhaps nowhere, in this library? Initially, I had tried to search for this manuscript in an area remote from the psychobiology sections. If someone had meant to conceal the book, and not steal it, the book would probably be farthest from the place that one would expect it to be. I did that, to no avail. The next day, I looked for it in any section in which one would expect Sullivan's monograph: psychology, metaphysics, sociology, and so forth. Although the reference librarian insisted that the professor's monograph would be in the psychobiology section, I was still obligated to look elsewhere. No luck, again. On the third day, I felt tired and dejected. I was questioning my intentions and my need to find the key to the Man's life. Had I really grown this obsessed that I could not even focus on my graduate dissertation? Why was I drawn to this Man, of whom I knew so little? I had surely grown insane, and the Man was slowly drawing me into his quiet madness. There was nowhere to go, but where this book was leading me. I couldn't stop now. I had relinquished all control.

Dearest Mallory,
Your cardiac resuscitation was difficult. That's true. I hope you realize this. We did all we could. You must understand. Stephen and I tried, but at the end, you decided it was too much for you. The burnt skin and the broken ribs, it was all too much. They were excessive, even for you, who tended to show no emotion. Even if you couldn't tell us, I could tell. Telepathy may occasionally exist between twins. Occasionally. I think you had already made that decision when you came to the hospital. That you must go, somewhere, that you must leave this place. You couldn't stay here a minute longer. Your place was elsewhere. You had decided your fate years earlier, with the severe depression that haunted you. Your Prozac eyes were deceiving. When awake, your eyes shone and revealed the bright, cheery Mallory you weren't. When asleep, your eyes would have that slow-rolling movement characteristic of someone with depression. Now, you looked like a burnt mannequin, so unreal, like a monster we'd seen in a horror film, your eyes bulging and red. I'm sorry to mention this, but your face looked like Leatherface's, the masked killer in *The Texas Chain Saw Massacre*. (Do you remember that horror film when we first snuck downstairs furtively and watched it on HBO, while eating popcorn and drinking Father's whiskey?) But unlike Leatherface, you were solemn and reposed on the hospital's gurney. You didn't wield a chainsaw. You didn't demand justice. You didn't flail that saw in the air

in anger and defeat when your last victim, that Final Girl
Sally escaped. You were the killer's victim, not the killer
himself. As I said before, you were not made for this world.
Perhaps you wanted to return to the galaxy from which
you originally came. That would explain a lot. When they
wheeled you into the ER, a little girl who had accompanied
her mother to the emergency department screamed when
looking at you. Once a beauty queen, you had turned into
a literal monster, a Leatherface. I felt for you. In your own
eyes, you were your own Leatherface, though. I had known
that for a long time. I hadn't done anything about it.

    Regretfully,

    Morgan

VINCENT DUCHENE

Vincent's hemoptysis is worsening. He is now measuring his bloody sputum. It's a cup more than the prior week. He methodically measures it. He reluctantly smells its acrid aroma. He is used to blood but not his. His breathing is more labored now. Vincent is gasping for air regularly. Death is not far behind, he thinks. He'll have several months of life but not much more. He is surprisingly content.

At fifty years of age, he has lived a full life. A lonely life for most of it when his wife died almost ten years ago, three years after his marriage to her. The stress over her death had caused physical damage. He had developed stress-induced cardiomyopathy. He was literally heart-broken. He couldn't live with anyone else, so he had lived a solitary existence since that time. He endured his loneliness in the hospital working as a surgeon for long hours. He endured it in the company of his surgical residents. The residents were his lifeline. He would be dead without them.

Vincent has lived with his late wife's ghost in an empty, large home. In the large home, he has sequestered himself in a cubular room, which he doesn't leave much. For the past several months, he has fixated on the figure of a pregnant and dying woman, Nadia, who is the same age as he is. She keeps him calm. Someone else is feeling what he is feeling. Someone else will have gone before him. Someone else will experience a similar death before he does.

He has been unable to see Nadia for the last week. It

appears that she has moved into another room. He cannot make out any shadows beyond the laced curtains. Has she been moved to a hospital? Is she dying soon? Will she give birth before she dies? These questions hover in his mind, constantly, obsessively. He has grown so tired thinking of Nadia. So tired! But he also believes that she is keeping him alive. He has something to live for now, someone to occupy his time.

Nadia has returned to her room. Looking beyond the lace curtains, Vincent sees her shadowy presence in her bed. She is quieter now, lying still. Vincent has moved his bed into the sitting room, from which he continues to glimpse her. He has lost all energy. He feels his cancer spreading, a cancer that has become a friend. He has been so alone since his wife died. He returns to bed. He looks at Nadia's lace curtains again. He finds some comfort within those curtains. He slowly drifts to sleep.

A week after the Man's sudden disappearance, as I was re-reading an article on Poe's *The Fall of the House of Usher*, I noticed a reference to Poe's other story, *The Purloined Letter*. Of course! In trying to find the book in an elaborate hiding or misplaced space, I had forgotten to look for it in plain sight. I was reminded that sometimes you can't see things that are too close to you. The myopic gaze. I went back to the shelf where the monograph was initially placed, and, to my tempered amazement, I found the mysterious manuscript that had led me on this quest. I was imagining this to be the holiest of grails. I reasoned that on the day the Man and I had both been looking for the monograph, it had been misplaced. And, on the subsequent day, the librarian had returned the manuscript to its proper place without realizing it. I, however, had already formed the notion that it was lost or misplaced, and began looking for it elsewhere. I now imagined myself as the fictional detective, C. Auguste Dupin of Poe's tale, and began to imagine the mystery that lay before me.

1996 | NORFOLK, MASSACHUSETTS
MORGAN DUCHENE

Twin Sister,

Let's go back to the birth canal, where everything began. You were born two minutes ahead of me. In the scheme of things, it's not a long time. But, during conception, that two minutes means everything. Every second is a second of oxygen from which one's deprived. You were given more nutrients. You occupied the dominant position. You were superior. That is no doubt why you excelled in beauty, why you were considered the daughter whom Father favored. If we were in England and part of the monarchy, you would have the birthright of the first born, the opportunity to inherit family fortunes, even entire kingdoms. Scientists have theorized that first-born children have more self-esteem and higher IQs, while lastborns tend to be lazy and irresponsible. Psychologist Alfred Adler, Freud's contemporary, even theorized how a child's position within the family would actualize in their personality. As the oldest, you had to learn to share. Parental expectations were high. You were given responsibility and expected to set an example. I think that's mainly true. You were certainly smarter than I was. Sure, I became a doctor, but that was because of hard work and not of natural abilities, something that you wouldn't understand. But, along with being the firstborn, the burden of responsibility fell on you. We had no mother, but in your own way, you were a mother figure. You carried the albatross of the family, the dead weight that none of us could cast off. You saw Father that day, and his death killed you. I know that now. Your guilt was written over it, but I was responsible for it all. As the first born, you felt that it was your duty to reconcile that mistake. And you did, with its disastrous consequence. I'm sorry, again, Mallory. You must believe me.

XX,

Your twin

1996 | PROVIDENCE, RHODE ISLAND
THURSTON KAFKA

I slowly opened the monograph, rapt by the suspense and excited about the future it held for me. It felt so magical and alive. I could sense its hands hold my hands as I opened it. Its fingers were miniature and smooth, but they were guiding mine, as if they had mastery over my larger and coarser hands. I shivered. My hands trembled, in awe of this mysterious text that remained such a puzzle to me. It was an ordinary monograph, yet it seemed to exude such foreignness. Its pages smelled old, as if the book had been transported from a world that did not, and could not, exist. The smell was acidic, but there was an alkaline pungency to it. Was it blood that I smelled? It was so difficult to discern, but its smell was not redolent of anything that I had smelled before. It appeared that this text was an original autobiographical account of Sullivan's last days before she passed. It was no wonder that the Man was so bent on finding this, but he must have had a purpose. Its title was *Élan Vital: A Study in Life Unexplained*. I was not very familiar with Sullivan's oeuvre, as she discussed more science-related phenomenon than I cared to study. She had dispensed most of psychology for biology, which was a disappointment to me. However, the Man had piqued my interest in Sullivan's work, and, so, I continued reading.

In it, only a short preface remained, in which Sullivan had outlined her reasons for writing this manuscript, while the rest of the pages were torn and missing. Who would do such a thing with an original manuscript? This was unheard of at The Hay, where things were safeguarded for posterity. Nevertheless, I continued to review the monograph's preface, even more intrigued now. I was trying to read so carefully when the librarian slid toward me, like a slow, hissing snake, catching me off guard. She was hovering over me, looking at the text, and then pulled the manuscript from my anxious hands. Her expression was stern, and she then scolded me for defacing the University's property. *You could be dismissed from Brown for such an act,* she told me. *But I didn't do this,* I quickly retorted. *I found the monograph in this condition.* She remained silent for a few seconds, and then asked, "*Where is your accomplice? That Man who you were hanging around with. Where is he? It's suspicious that he is no longer here, and the pages of that book are missing.*" She made a valid point, and I quickly realized that he must have torn the pages when I was not looking, and then disappeared. I didn't know how to respond. I said, "*I know nothing about that. I didn't even really know him.*" She looked me sternly in the eyes, and I didn't wince, realizing that I must remain credible and trustworthy. She must have realized that I was telling the truth. "*Ok, I believe you,*" she continued. "*But, if you happen to see that man, retrieve those papers from him. The University will hear of this, and it may not bode well for you.*" I remained silent. The more I said, the guiltier I would appear. She had confiscated the monograph from me for evidentiary purposes. All my efforts had come to naught. I had failed. The Man had won. I had lost him.

Sis,

I'm this close to burning it all down. Why aren't you the fuck here when I need you the most? I hope you realize that you've abandoned me. I have no one here anymore. You and Father are gone. And I can't expect that you'll bail me out, once again. Do you remember that time when, as a bratty twelve-year-old, I had decided to defy the odds of being caught and had stolen two bags of Funyuns and two bottles of Pepsi from Rodriguez's bodega on Potters Ave.? (BTW, I think this may have may have my first manic episode before my official diagnosis of bipolar disorder.) I had meant to give the second set to you. But two of everything was too much for my little hands to muster. And, so, as I was running out of the store, the glass bottles fell and shattered. I then saw Mr. Rodriguez's avuncular eyes, the 74-year-old Guatemalan whom I had ridiculed with my petty theft, gaze at me. At that moment, I realized that I had killed whatever goodness he held for me. I had disgraced him, he who had made a life for himself here, with his own twins. But you were watching me all along and came to my rescue. Without a hitch, you went up to him and placed a five-dollar bill in his hand. You were taller than I was, so you were able to reach the counter more than adequately. You told him, "Sorry, Mr. Rodriguez, I think my sister was in such a hurry to leave the store that she forgot to pay you." He didn't question this fib. You had a way of convincing anyone about anything. No one could read into your occasional lies, even I. Mr. Rodriguez didn't take your money. "It's all right, dear," he said. "The bottles of Pepsi are broken anyway. You don't have to pay for something that you can't drink." He then went to the large fridge in the back of the store and gave you two new Pepsi bottles. "Muchos gracias," you had told him. And his face shone like he had seen an angel. "Of course, mi querida," he had replied to you. Then you calmly walked toward me and whisked me out of the store. I had never felt so embarrassed in my life. But you had come to my rescue like some angel from above. I'm pretty sure that you're a real angel now, with those glowing white wings that you always wanted, dear sister.

xx,
Sister

Part II
MORGAN
& CHERRY

I don't look like your average first-year Emergency Room resident physician. Cropped, jet-black hair; a small, silver nose ring; a pasty face, dry and white as bone. That is me. If we fucked, you'd glimpse a tattoo of a magnolia on my right inner thigh, courtesy of Seaport Tattoo on Dorchester Avenue during a drunken spree in college. If you saw me in a hallway somewhere, you could mistake me for a depressively aloof goth girl. You would undoubtedly think I was a bitch. I'm no wallflower. I don't blend in nicely. I stand out in a crowd. You'd pick me out of a lineup with ease. Despite appearances, I was damn good at my job. I could intubate a patient better than the attending physicians at the hospital, and my lumbar punctures were considered golden champagne taps, every single time. I'm probably getting ahead of myself here, but I have so much time now to reflect on all these things while in prison, awaiting trial for murder. I don't want you to sympathize with me or feel sorry for me, because I'm beyond that. I would probably do it again if given the chance. I have a higher purpose now. I'm waiting for her to come and save me.

Let's talk about that night. It may have been my reaction to the burn victim who was abruptly wheeled into the trauma unit. Perhaps it was the way my sweat struck her forehead and quickly absorbed into it, like warm butter on dry, burnt toast. It was like a slow-motion film that had instantaneously turned real. My sweat had been the catalyst that started it all, the impetus that had turned on the projector and started this horror film. I had Death, the film's director, to thank for this. But there is more time to talk about what's real and what's not, about what Death is and what it isn't. I promise.

But, first, the victim's face. That face! It was beautifully tragic once, what you would see in the silent, pantomimic black-and-white films of the 1920s. It had now been scorched. It resembled a desert, where once stood a city with walls and borders. The pulsing vein along her hairline had always reminded me of the map of the Missouri river, with the brightest azure water. It was that river that had differentiated me from her. It was the Missouri river along her hairline that had separated our states. My jagged and extraneous Floridian border to her smooth one. It had made me appreciate her as someone other than myself. Although I hadn't seen her pulsing vein since Father's funeral over eight years ago, I recognized it instantaneously, as if it were a part of my own body.

But now the vein was beating distantly, its currents receding. The river had dried. The nose had merged with the mouth. The eyelids and eyebrows had become one. Everything had congealed together, everything had dried. Rivers were on fire. Mountains had crumbled. Fortresses were taken. The city had been ransacked. Her face had lost the battle. A fire had eventually triumphed in this acrid war.

When she was first wheeled into the ER, the doctors would've tried to placate her, to mitigate her ceaseless screaming. They would've told her to calm down when they themselves had probably never experienced the death of nerves, those relay stations that are both sensitive and resilient. They would have sedated her with Ativan or Propofol. (This is assuming she wasn't comatose when she arrived here.) They would've felt compassion for her, an unfortunate woman in her mid-twenties who still had so much life to live, so much more to give. The good ones would've empathized with her. All would have tried to save her. But, in the end, they would realize that fire always wins, that things get lost in fires, that salvage is rarely possible when a fire is implicated. From that moment on, I would begin to think of things that I could lose in future conflagrations. In my mind, fires would continue to blaze and raze those whom I loved or cared about.

To see yourself on another's face at the moment of their death is nothing you could prepare for. It is something unimaginable, something otherworldly, especially when ancestral blood is at issue. It's to see yourself dead while you're living. It's to see your future self, a self that has deserted you. I call it another version of a memento mori, death-in-life, or life-in-death. You select that unfortunate, fucking choice.

Let me explain. It was 11:11 pm when I was called into the emergency department. The witching hour, as I like to call it when all good and strange things come your way. A time when anything you wish for is theoretically possible, a time when I can cast my black spell to make everything right again. I know this is not technically the definition of a witching hour, but, for me, it was supernaturally extraordinary. In my case, as an Emergency Room resident, it's a lucky time. It's the time when I start discharging patients. It's when everything bad suddenly turns good. That hour was my good fortune. It worked for me. It was my lucky, black charm.

I was high and fucked up that night, not from any drugs, but from my mind. I have bipolar disorder type I, you should know, and had not taken my meds that night, once again. You could say I had forgotten, but that wasn't really the case. I hated how lithium made me feel. I despised its control over me. Drugged and anxious, I felt dull with that substance coursing through my veins. I had developed a tremor in my hands from having taken it all these years. The tremor would make me drop things. I would have an arduous time performing medical procedures. I had lost a great deal of hair, too, hair that once had been thick and voluminous. I now resorted to wearing semi-cheap wigs, wigs that made me look like the whore I was. I also abhorred the taste of that drug. That metallic flavor had eviscerated my taste buds, so I could no longer taste and smell the food I loved. It had affected my day-to-day duties as an emergency physician. To put it bluntly, I fucking loathed it. I wished to destroy the entire arsenal of that compound into smithereens.

As fate would have it, I was the unfortunate ER-resident on-call that night. (The magic hour was not so magical that night, to say the least.) I had decided to stay at the hospital. My commute was too far. Massachusetts General

Hospital was in the East End neighborhood while I lived in Cambridge. On a good day, the commute would take half an hour. On a bad day, it could be close to an hour. As a first-year resident who had to respond to calls urgently, I neither had the time nor the equanimity to be able to respond as I should if I were not close to the hospital.

If not high on my mind, I was high on marijuana, methamphetamine, or cocaine, my drugs of choice. Joe, a 19-year-old orderly at the hospital was my connection. He would supply me with whatever I needed there, which was usually marijuana. If I were in a depressed state, cocaine was more desirable but cost more. In my manic state, when I had severe insomnia, marijuana calmed me the fuck down and made me warmly likable. ER residents living in Boston are not particularly rich. We can barely scrape by as it is. A rumor had circulated that there was a large presence of drug trafficking in the hospital and that an Irish-Italian gang was the orchestrator. If there was, I never questioned Joe about it. At times, I could see him on the verge of a breakdown, as if this were all a little too much for him. Believe me, you don't mess with any Irish-Italian gangs here. I was just happy to get my drugs. To each their own.

One time, a resident in neurology had seen me smoke weed and inquired about my dealer. I didn't want to implicate Joe, so I acted as the go-between and, on occasion, sold the resident some. It wasn't ideal, but I knew that I could be blackmailed if I didn't comply. Of course, the rest didn't know anything about this, and if they did, they never confronted me. I was not one to be confronted. I could kick the shit out of anyone who dared to suppress or challenge me, verbally or intellectually. I was the devil in disguise. I was the witch they feared to defy. I was their absolute fucking nightmare.

I have a lot of time now to think about what happened that night and the subsequent days. Sitting here in my oversized, orange jumpsuit, with the name Bay State Correctional Center emblazoned in bold lettering, I think about her all the time. I think about Cherry, while I doodle her enigmatic face in this tattered journal. She showed me a glimpse of an extraordinary life that I had not seen before. I'll know she'll return for me and tell me in her dry, monotone voice, "You did it for me, for us, Morgan. My body is proof."

CHERRY

She smelled like three a.m. It was a musty odor, one that was difficult to discern. A mixture of stale smoke and bad perfume came to my mind, but it was something more pungent. It was a smell that didn't seem to originate from any place that was familiar. It was primitive. It sharpened one's sense. It reeked of unrequited love. In short, the smell was extraordinary but not in a good way.

She was a mess, too. Her hair was disheveled, resembling a bird's nest. Some of it was haphazardly tied with a rubber band. Partial eyeliner was hurriedly and clumsily drawn on her lower eyelid. She had not shaved her arm hair. Her white tank top, the wife beater, was strewn with blotches of blood. She wore a tattered bra. It smelled of sweat and sadness. She looked sixty, although she was ten years younger. Several days ago, she had attempted to hand scissors to a stranger and asked him to make her look less like herself. "Make me look less like Cherry," she had told him. "Make me look less like myself." As expected, the stranger had refused the scissors and told her, "You've got some serious problems, lady. You'd have better luck with a psychiatrist than those shears. I suggest you get yourself some help."

Cherry presented to the emergency department with her blood. She wiped this crimson fluid from her vagina. She then raised her right bloodied hand and displayed it to the ER clerk. It was as if she were taking an oath at trial and testifying to the accuracy of the bleeding. The blood was the evidence. Her raised hand was the attestation. "I'm hemorrhaging," she would dispassionately say to the clerk, a robust, no-nonsense woman who was used to seeing many medical monstrosities—semi-amputated dangling hands; pipes shoved into anuses; hair that had been plucked, shaped into a small ball, and then consumed. She had seen many things but, somehow, this one gesture caught the clerk off-guard. The clerk would later state to the investigators that it was the manner which the woman calmly wiped the blood from her vagina in plain sight, smiled, smelled it, and showed it to her that made this even more horrific than anything she had seen before, more surreal than an axe to the head, more devastating than an amputated arm, more personal than sex. The patient called herself Cherry, though, later, no one would be able to verify if this is who she really was. She didn't provide a last name, either, but checked herself into the emergency department with a complaint of vaginal hemorrhaging. "I'm hemorrhaging," she again said, even more calmly than before.

Stunned, the clerk immediately motioned Cherry to the medical assistant who took the woman's vitals. "We've got a bleeder," the clerk relayed. She was still amazed at the sight and equanimity of this patient. The medical assistant would also later suggest to the investigators from the health department that "something was not right." "I couldn't put my finger on it at the time, but something was just not right, you know? It was like she was from a different place and time than us. Does that make sense?"

Cherry continued, again, even more nonchalantly: "My

name is Cherry, red like the blood that is flowing from my vagina. If someone could make it all stop, I would really appreciate it." "Of course, we'll do all we can, honey" the assistant quizzically murmured, though the smell of the putrid blood was gagging her. "We'll do our best. You just need to sit back and relax, dear." But Cherry was already relaxed, to the point where she didn't care what happened to her. She could hemorrhage that blood to the point of death, and she would be fine with that.

The patient's blood pressure was elevated, which didn't make sense in this circumstance. The assistant couldn't make any sense of it, although it was reassuring that volume loss wasn't a problem. The assistant would later vouch that "it was so weird, you know, like everything you have seen and learned has been turned upside down. Like you don't where you stand anymore." "It was very weird," she would repeat.

Where were we? I'm so disoriented these days, with every fucking thing that happened that night. I think I was discussing it, that night that will forever pierce me, that will eventually cause me to experience post-traumatic nightmares among every other condition that I have. Wasn't I? They wheeled the victim in a gurney from the entrance of the ER and placed her in trauma room 1 that I had been assigned. I was the junior resident on-call. I loved trauma. It made me feel like the bad-ass doctor I was.

The night had been going well. It wasn't particularly busy, but something seemed out of character. I had a feeling that things were about to go south, but it was just an intuition. First, it was an unusually cold summer night in Boston. The coffee pot was also empty in the ER station, which rarely happens. I live off caffeine. All residents do. Otherwise, I could never outlive the night and be able to care for my patients. I especially liked hospital coffee, because it wasn't particularly good, but it didn't pretend to be anything more. You got what you got. You knew where you stood with it, unlike other complications in life. Lately, I'd also been supplementing caffeine with modafinil. For me, it didn't provide any of those magical attributes that it promises—mental acuity and alacrity—although it made it more difficult to fall asleep. I felt cheated that I didn't experience those benefits, but I was at least grateful that I could stay awake. I should add that I obtained these meds illegally. But I didn't take them when I was in a manic state, so please don't admonish me. Provigil isn't to be taken by those with bipolar disorder (especially during a manic cycle) but Barry, our friendly drug rep at the hospital, supplied me with what I needed. He would ask for a fuck, now and then, and I obliged. It was only fair. Drugs for sex. Isn't that how the rest of the outside world functioned? The hospital shouldn't be any different, I reasoned.

Let's get back to the story. They wheeled her into Trauma 1. She was a burn victim but would be evaluated first by the trauma team. This was done to see if there were other medical issues before the extensive burns were attended to. Everything had become so routine that I never even bothered with the logistics of what had brought the victim into the unit. For me, the backstory was less important than what was occurring at the present. I was for the here-and-now rather than for the past. One had control over the present. The past was gone. "Move on, people," is my mantra. There's nothing left to see when things have already happened. Move on, before the juggernaut runs you over.

I had heeded the lessons of the angel in Paul Klee's famous painting, *Angelus Novus*. That angel who is so fixated on the past that the storm of progress hurls it into a future over which it has little control. Control was my lifeline. Control was the only thing that made me sane and grounded. Without it, I would perish into the mess of a disastrous history.

And that's when I saw that face. My identical twin sister Mallory's beatific face. Our facial features were the same, but she was the angel while I was her twin counterpart, the devil who had secretly despised her. She would have been the ideal sister had I not been so fucked up by my bipolar disorder, depressed and manic over every misunderstanding that occurred between us while growing up together. She was the feminine counterpart to my masculine ego. She loved everyone while I always found a reason to hate. She gave while I took, depleting everything in sight. In short, she was love while I was hate.

But, now, while looking at her, while looking at myself, I felt a purity that I had not experienced before. She was scorched earth. She was a gasoline tank with a match. She was a forest fire, set off by an arson. But I realized that I loved her, had loved her so much. I had only hated her because I hated myself. I had loathed her features because those were my features, too. I was never one for crying but, at that moment, tears welled in my eyes to the point of sobbing, had I not restrained myself. I realized that I cared only for her, my only living relative since my father's death five years ago. If I had a mother, I would've gone crying to her and clasped her tightly, too tightly. "Don't leave me, Mother," I would say. "I have no one now. I have no connection to this world, except for you. Please stay." I would have said all of this to her, had she been around. But she had vanished after I was born, and my father had said that she was good as dead. Mallory and I had not inquired. Father's love was enough for both of us. Father was the only savior we needed. But now that Mallory was gone, I needed Mother, wherever and whoever she was.

In looking at Mallory, I felt that I had been staring at her for an hour, but only a few minutes had elapsed. Although she was horrifically burned, I still saw that face. That face! The Missouri River along her flawless hairline. (She had an alluringly handsome widow's peak. I always thought this signified that she would outlive her husband if she married. I would be wrong.) The beautiful, perfectly sculpted mole. Those insanely immaculately plucked eyebrows that looked authentic and natural. The aquiline, sharply sculpted nose that reminded me of some Greek goddess, Aphrodite, perhaps.

Sure, I had those same features, but on my face, it all looked so plain, as if they never belonged there. My frame couldn't encapsulate that beauty. It looked like a fucking mess. I was a counterfeit painting next to her original. It was as if something were always off with me: the nose that wasn't exactly perfect, the eyebrows that were a little peaked, and my hair, yes, let's talk about. I had shorn it when I was in high school and had kept it that length since. It was also dyed jet black, like some gothic misfit, who was always trying to stay aloof and make life quietly miserable for everyone. Hers was gloriously blonde and full, and, when she walked, it naturally followed her, like a train on a wedding gown. As I mentioned, the lithium that I was taking had caused my hair to thin—I had developed alopecia—and my hair was never going to be the same.

However, despite the differences in our hair length and color, and even if she had planted her hair on my head, our features, though similar, would never be the same. I would always be the bad copy, the simulation, while she would be the original article, pristine and unaltered. I would always be a shitty counterfeit, no matter how hard I tried. Who would have thought the counterfeit would outlive the original? Who would've thought that a drug-addicted girl with bipolar disorder and so many vices would outlive her perfectly minted twin sister? Well, the world is a crazy place. But you didn't really know my sister, did you? I'll get to that soon.

While I still saw Mallory's beauty underneath the burns, her features had melted and coalesced together. Her nose had flattened. Her eyebrows were singed and truncated. The Missouri River had dried. She no longer had hair, that glorious hair. Her skin, which had been so pale and pure, was now charred. She had drifted into another world but was still with us, on the border. I would attempt to pull her back, pull her towards me. I would tell her how much I loved her, how I would do anything for her if she just survived this blow. I needed her to survive because she needed to hear those words. Those words would make us sisters again. Twin sisters. But I somehow knew this was her farewell, her swan song, a beautiful tune she would sing before she passed. She was leaving a remnant of her beauty with me to carry forward, this last vestige of hers, a trace of who she once was.

At that moment, I thought of the Bauhaus song that Mallory and I used to sing together as seniors in high school before we parted ways and never saw one another again. It was the band's most unassuming and delicate track on its album, *The Sky's Gone Out*, with its acoustic guitar and plucked bass. It's as if Peter Murphy had wanted the song to remain concealed among the oeuvre's chaos. The song's first line had become our mantra: "All we ever wanted was everything." We were both destined for great things and nothing could stop us, we believed. We wanted to conquer it all. New York City. Hollywood. Miami. Nothing was insurmountable. Nowhere was out of reach. Mallory and I, however, had consciously decided to remove the line that came after that sentence: "All we ever got was cold," and instead croon our way into the chorus line, "Oh, to be the cream; oh, to be the cream." And, at that time, at the height of our intelligence and beauty, we thought we were that fucking cream.

Sill in a reverie of that chorus and that memory, I heard a distant, reverberated sound, "Morgan, we need to intubate her. I hear distant breathing." It was the chief resident, Stephen, who was oblivious to the entire situation. I hadn't told anyone about Mallory, and her face was so badly scorched that no one could guess she was my twin sister. I was private that way. "Get the intubation kit," he continued. "More fluids, too. She's becoming bradycardic. Get the crash cart ready. Epinephrine. Nurses, stand by." But I wanted to tell Stephen this was hopeless, although he somehow knew it, too. *She's flying away, like an angel,* I wanted to say, *like a star that's bleeding and burning. Like an imploded stellar body, a deadstar. Let her go. Let her go.* But Stephen wasn't ready yet. He had not given up hope, as I had. Though I pretended I was strong, Stephen was stronger in his silent and awkward way. His shoulders told the story that he could not convey by his brevity and social awkwardness. But I had already lost hope. Like dominoes, once this hope falters, the rest follow. And my hope had faltered. There were no dominoes left standing.

As if Mallory could hear and respond to me, she went into v-fib, her heart signaling us to hear her pleading. It was a message from her to me: *"Morgan, please tell him to stop. You know that I'm ready to see Father. You can join us later. But now it's my turn. I'll see you when you get here. I'll see you when you're ready."*

"The crash cart," Stephen yelled to the nurses. "Epinephrine, paddles. Get everything ready. She's in v-fib." But it was already too late. The flat line on the heart monitor told us so. Her message had been so clear. She had crossed the border and left me behind it. She had flown or sailed away home, or maybe to Tahiti, a place where she had always wanted to go since we were children. I wanted to tell her then, *"Sister, maybe we'll go to Tahiti. Yes, maybe we'll go to Tahiti. Someday, together, where fires won't consume us, where waves will carry us away."*

EMERGENCY MEDICAL RESPONDER NOTE

Response to an anonymous call. Dispatched to a burning apartment in Brookline, MA, where the body of a young woman was found. Clothes were cut with scissors and removed. Face and body with fourth-degree burns affecting deeper tissue and organs. Singed nasal and eyebrow hairs. The total burn surface area (TBSA) is estimated to be 54%. Elapsed time from the burn is likely one hour. Respiratory compromise is evident. Field intubation and bag-valve ventilation was undertaken. Glasgow Coma Score of 6, as patient is responsive to pain and makes incomprehensible sounds but, otherwise, is comatose. The patient is hypotensive with a blood pressure of 70/50 mm Hg. The heart is tachycardic at 125 bpm with a normal rhythm. Lung sounds prior to intubation were coarse, with stridor. Pulmonary edema is likely. Intubation is successful. Large-bore IV catheter placed for fluid administration with crystalloid solutions to increase blood pressure. Dry sterile bandages were placed on large burns, although this will likely not be sufficient to prevent infection. Call made to Massachusetts Hospital. The patient was accepted to the trauma unit and burn center. Condition is extremely critical.

Moments after Mallory departed, I was still staring at her face. Stephen, however, was absorbed in the technicality of his duties: *"Time of death: 12:14 am. Nurses, please give me her medical file, so I can call her next of kin. She may be an organ donor, but we can't use any of her body parts. Such a shame. We did everything we could. We truly did."* He paused various times, while delivering his monologue, as if he didn't know whether he should stop or continue. I think that Stephen wanted some validation from me that he had given all he had. He then terminated his speech, and suddenly turned to me and said, *"Morgan, don't take it so hard. We did our best."* This gesture caught me off guard for a moment because I hadn't shown any response as Mallory was coding. I wanted to tell him *I know we did because she was destined to go.* But I just remained quiet and nodded my head.

Poor Stephen. I knew that deep inside he felt that he was somewhat responsible for Mallory's demise, that it was that little thing that he had not anticipated, that trivial aspect that he had overlooked, which could have saved her. Not enough epinephrine, not enough fluids, not enough volts for the defibrillator. I wanted to touch Stephen's cheek with my frigid hands and tell him, *I love you for wanting to save my sister so badly. She was just a stranger to you, yet you did just as much for her as I would. Mallory would go, with or without you.* I wish I could tell him this. But I had a reputation to uphold at this teaching hospital. I could never let Stephen see my vulnerability, my Achilles' heel. I just responded in my usual, flippant way: *"Next time, it'll be better. We know the statistics on burns. Let's take a break."* Stephen looked at me, in a daze, thinking how I could be such an uncaring bitch in such a situation. But my reputation preceded me, so he just gave up on that thought and carried on. He was an absolute gentleman.

I went in a separate direction, contemplating my next move. Wouldn't they attempt to decipher Mallory's identity? Wouldn't they try to find her next of kin and stumble upon me? What if they did? Why was I so protective? Why was I this way, so private? I hadn't told anyone about my twin sister, but why? There wasn't a reason to hide it, but to address it now seemed so irrelevant and suspicious. My greater concern now was Mallory's death. Her presentation at the hospital had devastated me. Minutes ago, I could not even think about the situation surrounding her death. But, now that she had passed, my thoughts veered to the circumstances of her death. How did she burn? Was this a case of arson in which she was unfortunately caught? Was this murder? Who would identify her body? I assumed it would be her roommate in Boston.

I then recalled the conversation that I had had with our mutual high school friend, Jenny O., on the phone a few weeks ago. She had told me that Mallory recently returned from New York City and relocated to Boston. She apparently was living with a roommate in Brookline. But I hadn't inquired further. "Aren't you interested to know what happened to your sister's modeling career?" Jenny had asked me. "Not really," I had disinterestedly replied. "Well, let's just say it didn't go so well. She did one Gap ad campaign and then her career just fizzled. Wilhelmina Models in New York City flat out rejected her, saying she was too old for the agency. Isn't that super sad?" Jenny rambled. And then I recognized what had caused my sister's death, what had charred her to death. I guess I had always known, but I didn't know it would be this devastating. She had told me so, long ago, through her actions. My thoughts went everywhere and nowhere at the same time. I had hit rock bottom, but I still had depths to go before the abyss.

Throughout the years, this is what I've learned. For your life to fall apart, it doesn't matter if you're in a swanky restaurant, in a bank being held hostage, or in a casino spinning a roulette wheel with chips stacked at your side. It can fall apart in an instant in either the best or worst of circumstances, whether you're rich or poor. Life is a Russian roulette. Each day, you're loading a bullet in a chamber of a revolver. Each day, you're spinning the cylinder. Each day, you're pulling the trigger, wherever you may be. There's no reason, then, why your life can't get fucked up in any one place. The spin, executed by my friend Death that night, determined it all. My life unraveled at the entrance to Trauma 1 in the emergency department. It fell apart before I had a chance to evaluate and rectify it. When you've touched the sky, like Icarus once did, the fall is colossal. In moments like these, you begin to feel Death creeping in and you know nothing will ever be the same. Death had not given me a signal of what it had planned for me that night. It had simply barged in, at my most vulnerable and depressed state, and pulled the trigger. It had thrown a stone in a pond long away from here. I was just now feeling the ripples.

Nostalgia can be seductive. We find it difficult to vanquish memories because we think they're happy moments. But these memories are not happy. These memories are not sad. They simply are. The mind just has a peculiar way to turn these memories into something palatable, so that we find some truth, some glimmer of a history that we once thought important and sentimental. It's a way to make the past idyllic, to make the past seem easier than we knew it was. It's a method to trick our minds into thinking that we had it a lot easier then, that this halcyon place still exists. But this Shangri-La doesn't exist. It never did. At least for me.

When Mallory died just moments ago, my thoughts were static. They were not moving. But they returned, slowly. They flooded me like a violent thunderstorm after a drought. My twin sister had always jokingly mentioned that I leave dead bodies behind me wherever and whenever I go. At first, I would laugh to humor her. Her statement was preposterous, I thought. But her observation lingered until I couldn't doubt it anymore. I really do leave bodies by the wayside, I thought. I give bodies to Death itself who is always one step behind me to make sure that I somehow fuck things up. Then he collects them. Death follows me. It anticipates my every move. It listens to everything I say. It's an informant. I can never win when it's around. It gathers intel mud uses this against me. It had used this ammunition against Mallory. I'm sure of it.

By instinct, human beings always choose to side with the weaker—the weaker individual, the weaker company, the weaker animal. We feel connected to the weaker, the underdog because that's who we are inside. All of us, even in the best of our days, are weaker. I now know this to be true. I had always shunned the weak, the timid, because to admit this was to give it validity. To me, Mallory was weak, and I always attempted to be the person who she wasn't. I thought that her weakness resided in her goodness to others, her absolute self-sacrifice for anything and to anyone. She was revered in the community for this. Her weakness, however, lay deeper. As I will later recount, she had body dysmorphic disorder, and always struggled with this condition. With Mallory's death, however, I realized that I had projected this weakness onto others, and I was just as weak as anyone else. I just chose not to show it because I was masquerading. I was the weakest of them all because I was afraid to show my weakness, unlike Mallory who wore this on her sleeves.

They say that love can move worlds, that love can bridge gaps that remain suspended for eternity. But the truth is that hate can be just as strong, if not stronger. I should know because I began to hate Mallory at such an early age. I'll recount our history, the narrative that shaped who we were to become.

Mallory and I were born into rather ordinary circumstances, expect for the fact that we didn't have a mother. Plenty of children are born into such households and, because we didn't know any better, we didn't think much about the loss of a mother until much later. I don't have the best memory, either. You can blame it on my recreational drug use or bipolar disorder, or both.

My earliest memory is from age six. Mallory and I were celebrating our birthday. I remember the cake. It was a cake with a Barbie doll placed in it. The doll's clothing and hoop skirt were made of vanilla frosting. I can still picture both the Barbie and the taste of that frosting. That's when I knew I didn't like anything feminine. Our girl friends at that party were absolutely enamored of that cake. But I didn't care at all. I just wanted to make my wish and taste that damn cake.

As if you haven't guessed it already, I didn't like dolls, but Mallory adored them. She would amuse herself for hours by dressing them and coloring their hair with anything she could find around the house, whether this was Kool-Aid, beets, or Father's coffee grounds. My sister was inventive that way. Her manner of approaching things was delightful, resourceful, and creative. She would also simulate feeding her Barbies, dressing them in all sorts of clothes that my father, Vincent, bought for those dolls. Mallory named her favorite Barbie Melissa, another "M" that would be added to our household of "M's." That doll had a flair. She had shiny, voluminous blonde hair that reflected Mallory's physical attributes. I should've realized that at some point in her life, Mallory would want to become a high-fashion model, despite her extensive acumen and Ivy League education. She was destined for that lifestyle, and, frankly, she should have just immersed herself in that world from the beginning. From an early age, she carefully read fashion magazines, like *Vogue* and *Mademoiselle*, for hours at a time, as if they were encyclopedias of life. She aspired to be a high-fashion model, but she never made it. After we lost touch in college, I remember seeing her in a Gap campaign, featuring real people with interesting backgrounds. I thought she had found success, but nothing came of that campaign. I really wanted her to succeed in something that she had always wanted, but Mallory was always either too late or too early. Her modeling aspirations came too late and her death came too early. She sacrificed so much for everyone. Because Father was a highly respected surgeon, she didn't want to disappoint him, and, therefore, decided to embark upon an intellectual trajectory that would please him and satisfy her curiosity. Mallory would've made a great physician, too, although I don't think she would ever be able to handle the day-to-day grotesqueness, vomiting, and bleeding in the hospital. She was brought up to appreciate the finer and more delicate things in life, while I was born for defilement and shit. I knew that from any early age. Nothing could temper that fact.

Our names also set us apart. My Father had named me

Morgan after Morgan le Fay from the Arthurian legend, she who stirs up trouble between Arthur and his queen, Guinevere. Morgan le Fay learns of her magical powers from Merlin, and is depicted as fay, witch, and sorceress. In the later iterations of her in various medieval tales, she is illustrated as ambivalent, having attributes of both good and evil. As Father told me when I became a teenager, Morgan was a fitting name for me because I was his "enchantress." However, I always resented that he thought that I had evil in me, in addition to the good. I don't know if he named me because of this, but I think his labeling of me as Morgan was spot-on. He had a good intuition.

On the other hand, Mallory's name was selected by chance. Father was born in Germany and lived there prior to arriving in Providence, to matriculate at Brown University's medical school. His mother was German and his father French. He abhorred his mother's native tongue. He detested the harsh, guttural sound of that language and was always trying to smooth his English and German words into a more pleasant cadence. He had a penchant for anything French because he loved that language of love. He was endeared to Paris and had fond memories of it for the few times he had been there when he was younger. He didn't like to talk about his childhood or early adult life very much, and Mallory and I never inquired. His life as a surgeon was difficult enough at the hospital. As I would later come to know, Mallory's name was derived from the Old French maloret. Unbeknownst to Father, Mallory meant the unlucky one, the ill-omened. Father and I had a discussion of the origin of our names once and he almost gasped when I told him about the origin of my sister's name. "That's ridiculous," he said. "She is the most fortunate and lucky person I know." I felt hurt by this statement, mainly because he thought that I was not the most fortunate. But I knew what he meant. There was nothing malicious about his tone or statement. I now realize, though, that Mallory's name was particularly apt. She would be an unfortunate individual and die at a young age.

Who knew that I would be luckier than she was, if you call living luckier than dying? We have no control over the names that are given to us when we're born, but there is some truth to them. Morgan le Fay was a witch, and I considered myself as a sorceress, too. On the other hand, Mallory who was so refined and whose name was mellifluous sounding, was predestined for an untimely death. Father had selected our fates without realizing it.

I didn't sleep much those days when the acute phase of my bipolar disorder had set in. I had tried Ambien, Restoril, Klonopin, and whatever else I could obtain from either the automated dispensing units or drug closets at the hospital. If I were really desperate, the local drug rep would supply me with some of these medications. I was trying to stay away from the usual culprits, my go-to drugs of choice—cocaine and marijuana. I was taking one form of sleep medication almost every night now, which gave me a hangover the following day. In the mornings, like an addict, I would take Provigil to help combat my fatigue in the morning. If I felt more extravagant, I would purchase some cocaine, but that was rare. A resident's meager salary doesn't help. One night while at the hospital, I had even slept walked and rummaged the drug closet, as a nurse informed me the following morning. I thought that if I was ever caught in the drug closet without a good excuse, I could say I was sleepwalking. This particular nurse could vouch for me, I thought. It was an untenable and dangerous game I was playing. Taking a medication to sleep, which made me tired the next day, for which I had to then take something that would make me refreshed but jittery. I couldn't win. When I was younger, Father used to say that if I didn't sleep, someone else would steal my dreams. I don't wish that on anyone because, as far as I can remember, my dreams were always fucking lousy and grim.

Mallory's death has made me question existence itself. I was her darker counterpart, a darker ying to her lighter yang. We had grown up together, but our perception of everything was so different. She sought approval while I didn't give a fuck about anything. She was concerned about how others felt, and I, although a doctor, didn't give a shit about feelings. I know that's cold. I realize that's something to which I shouldn't confess, but that's just how I felt. I just wanted to do an adequate job and not kill anyone while on my shift. Mallory was emotional. I was technical, like a machine.

I first realized that Mallory had an issue with her body image during our teenage years. She was constantly asking me whether her nose was too small and slender, and whether her face was of the right proportion to accommodate that. Surprisingly, she didn't complain about her body much, although that was perfect, too. During our talks, I would look at her, perplexed and a little saddened. Was her self-esteem really that low? Mallory was considered the most unassumingly beautiful person in high school. There was no doubt about it. Everyone wanted to be her. Everyone wanted to fuck her. Everyone copied her hairstyle and clothes, without success. She was an original, but she never felt beautiful. The perception of herself was skewed, no matter how much I explained to her that she was perfect. I think I began hating her during those years because I felt that she was mocking me for being her bad copy. I believed that she was fishing for compliments, that she desired my validation. I no longer think that, but those lessons I learned will haunt me for years.

Later, during medical school, I realized that she had body dysmorphic disorder, and that only serotonin, cognitive behavioral therapy, and other treatments would help. She never tried any of those because she truly believed that she had flaws. She had the stubborn idea that treatments would just mask her inherent imperfections. Mallory had even consulted with a few plastic surgeons in the Boston area. Thankfully, they all said there was nothing they could do. That says a lot, considering that if surgeons can cut, they will, even if there's no reason to do so.

Mallory had special fixations on her nose and hair, both of which were flawless. Concerning her nose, she was always using a combination of foundations to make it appear larger than it was. I know that other girls were trying to make their noses smaller, but Mallory was convinced that her nose was minuscule. She felt like those cartoon characters, whose noses are depicted by a slant or a cone. Don't ask me the trick that she used because I never wear makeup, expect for an occasional eyeliner and lipstick. But Mallory knew the latest makeup tricks. She brought the latest products that the fashion magazines advertised. Although super intelligent, my sister was absolutely deceived by ads that would play into her dysmorphia. The way the advertising world validated her perceived flaws was pathetic. There was a correction for everything, even for my angelic sister's perfections.

Later, before we matriculated at college, Mallory at Brown and I at Boston University, I suggested that she consult a psychiatrist. Mallory was absolutely livid because she was convinced that a problem existed and that a psychiatrist would just attempt to conceal it instead of actually repairing it. She was normally such a composed and relaxed individual, but, when it came to her nose, she was absolutely blind and obnoxious. Besides looks, of which I was a bad replica, her only other similarity to me was her stubbornness that was specifically linked to her nose. At least, this tendency to be belligerent brought us together in a strange way.

In retrospect, I realize that I should have done much more for Mallory. One day, still in our teenage years, I accidentally saw her, with the bathroom door ajar, take a tweezer to her nostrils to enlarge the width. I was horrified at this sight. I came in, pretending that I had forgotten something, while giving her time to prepare for my arrival. "Where are you, Mallory? I think that I forgot my toothbrush in the bathroom." She stopped what she was doing. I didn't want her to feel more ashamed because of her perceived shortcoming, so I had taken my time to get to her. She quickly and unconsciously said, "I wish I could burn my face. My nose is so hideous." I looked at her, bewildered. "What did you say, Mallory?' I responded. "Oh, nothing," she said. "It was just a joke."

Yet, another time, during our senior year in high school, I saw her pluck out a small tuft of hair from the back of her head and eat it. This was such a sight! You had to be there to witness this lunacy. It was unbelievable that this was happening to my twin sister, who was considered so flawless and demure. She took that bit of hair, chewed it, and began to digest it. I immediately ran to her. I asked her what the hell she was doing. She was not surprised at seeing me, but instead said. "It's just hair, Morgan. I have so much of it. A haircut now and then doesn't hurt, does it?" "No," I answered, "a haircut doesn't hurt, but you're eating your fucking hair!" In her nonchalant but polite demeanor, she answered, "I get it. Thanks for being concerned about me, Morgan, but I know what I'm doing. It's just fun. It's something different. Don't worry. It won't happen again." She then took a bright red lipstick and began outlining and coloring her lips with it. I looked at her and walked away. Her hair-eating would happen again with disastrous consequences.

Several weeks later, Father received a call from The Miriam Hospital in Rhode Island notifying him that Mallory had been admitted for a minor endoscopic surgery for gastric outlet obstruction. At the time, I hadn't entered medical school, yet alone university, so I didn't know anything about her diagnosis. But Father had spoken to the ER doctor who told him that my sister had been diagnosed with a trichobezoar. When I asked Father what that meant, he told me in his usual calm and shy demeanor that the doctors had found pieces of ingested hair, coalesced into a ball, in Mallory's stomach. They had to perform surgery to remove this mass because it was blocking passage of food from her stomach to her intestines. Father, or Vincent as I was starting to call him by then, turned to me and said, "Morgan, do you know anything about this? Have you seen your sister eat her own hair?" Again, he never showed his anger, but I could tell that he wasn't pleased about what had happened to his golden-haired child. "No, Vincent, I haven't seen anything. Perhaps, she just pulled a bit of hair and then ate it. I think she used to do that when we were younger," I lied. Vincent replied, "Well, it's not nothing, Morgan, but I think she'll be fine. One of my colleagues in the hospital is performing the procedure on Mallory, so she should be all right for now. But, in the future, you need to tell me if you see anything suspicious. Anything. Got that? This could turn out to be something serious. And Mallory could really use her help in this." "Yes, for sure," I responded.

I had never had such a serious conversation with Vincent. I could tell that he was irked by this entire situation, but he didn't really believe that I was an accomplice, although he may have had a slight suspicion. My father had a medical condition of his own when he was younger, although he didn't really like to talk about it. During a casual conversation with one of his friends and colleagues a few years ago, I learned that he had a malignant lung cancer that remitted right before our birth. It apparently shocked the scientific community. Father was given a grim prognosis of death in a year and, then, just like that, the cancer was gone. He hadn't even considered chemotherapy given his prognosis, but then, suddenly, everything was copacetic again. Doctors attributed it to a variety of herbal supplements and lifestyle changes that Vincent had made during that time, but none of it made any sense. I wonder if Father was even diagnosed with cancer. I mean, how many stories have you heard where a patient emerges unscathed from a bad malignancy?

To return to Mallory's story, a psychiatrist consulted with her at the hospital, but given my sister's outlook on the entire situation, she never followed up with the doctor. And, surprisingly, Vincent never broached the topic again. They both wanted to suppress this incident and forget that it ever occurred. They desired to keep their blissful and untainted relationship intact.

After our father passed, my sister and I went to university and parted ways. That chapter of our lives had closed. In retrospect, Father was the glue who had bound our fucked-up lives. I don't know if Mallory continued to eat her hair again, but I doubt it. Mallory was smart that way. If she were caught, she would just change her plan and try something different. I wasn't with her when she decided to enter the world of modeling. That, too, was taken away from her. I should've known that her dysmorphia would worsen. And it did. It was a call for help that was a little too late. I had dismissed it and not taken it seriously enough. I'm certain that her failed modeling career was a sign that she was as ugly as she thought she was. Now I knew that she had deliberately burned her face.

I should tell you a little about my father and Mallory. They had a much closer relationship than I had with Vincent. I'm not ashamed of it, but Mallory was certainly the favorite of us two. Father adored her, but with both of us around, he felt guilty that he showered her with more compliments than he did with me. She was a perfect little girl, while I was considered a rebellious, goth child, with ripped Cure and Bauhaus t-shirts and thrashed Doc Martens boots. Perhaps I wanted to rebel because I knew I could never be loved by my father the way that he loved Mallory. Maybe it was a defense mechanism, a proactive move to rid myself of the pain I would feel if I competed with her on the same terms. If we were different, maybe it was the difference that he didn't like, I reasoned. That somehow made it psychologically easier to swallow. I don't know. Maybe. I shouldn't psychoanalyze this further. It won't get me far.

I could also see a darker side of Father that Mallory failed or refused to see. When he was around me, I could sense that he was a little afraid of me, as if I were reading his thoughts. He was so self-conscious, like a kid who's afraid to pet a dog for the first time, fearing his first bite. I didn't bite, but I felt that he thought I did. To me, Father was always a little too reserved and shy. He never dated anyone while we were growing up. I don't know if he missed what he had had with the mother I'd never know, or that he had had such a devastating time with all his previous relationships. It was as if he had a secret that he would not divulge to anyone, a secret that he thought I knew. But I didn't know and still don't know a fucking thing about him.

There was always this silent gap between us, a dead space that none of us dared to broach. I wanted to ask Vincent about it, but I knew that if I did, a floodgate would open and could never be closed. Right before his death, our conversation veered toward the owner of the home on 1111 Angell Street, adjacent to us. Having lived at our home until we left for college, Father and I never discussed that house, which seemed so dark and foreboding. I could tell that he wasn't eager to broach the topic, either. "By the way, Father, who owns that home next to us? I always assumed it would be demolished but someone owns it, right?" It took Vincent a few seconds to respond. He then replied, "You know, a few years before you and Mallory were born, a woman lived there alone. I don't think she had any family. Then, just like that, I heard she sold her home to a foundation and left for Europe."

I just looked at him. I don't know how he had fabricated this story, but it just didn't ring of the truth. For fuck's sake, a single woman who sells her home to a foundation and leaves for Europe. Really? Is that the best he could do? Were we dealing with a Gertrude Stein character here? His lie was blatant and clear, and he knew that I realized it, too. But why lie? All of us have secrets, and I knew this was his. Vincent then turned his back toward me and pretended that he had some work to do. "Morgan, I must get back to work now. I have a whole stack of reports to complete before the

heavy curtains to the trauma room. I was such a mess after Mallory's death minutes earlier. Cherry was lying on her back on a broken gurney. (The hospital had to make sacrifices during that time due to budgetary cuts. This was nothing new.) She was surprisingly calm unlike the other patients we usually see in the trauma unit.

However, she looked like a disaster, if I have to say so myself. I wasn't looking particularly great, but I looked presentable. Cherry, on the other hand, looked like she could not give a fuck about anything. The chart stated that she was fifty years of age, although she appeared much older. She had creases on her forehead and long vertical lines that laterally circumscribed her chin, what we in the medical field call Marionette lines. As a result, she looked unhappy, although this was only the effect of those creases. She had a blunted affect, a poker face. You couldn't read her if you tried. Her face was pale as bone, like she was seriously anemic. Her front teeth had sharp edges and were sooty. She was wearing a ripped, dirty, and cheap white tank top. Her nipples looked very prominent, as outlined by that thin top. The strap of her bra was partially torn, too. She had lined the bottom of her eyelid with a black eyeliner, which was now smudged. She was of mixed race, but you could tell that she had used white powder on her face to make herself appear milky. A minuscule tattoo that read "Cherry" in cursive writing was inscribed on her left wrist, as if she wanted to remember herself for herself only. I took this all in, as we physicians always do when we encounter patients. You'd be surprised if I told you that the smallest detail during an initial encounter with a patient can provide the biggest clue to a right diagnosis. The devil is in the detail, they say. The mysterious element is often hidden in those details. However, with Cherry, there was so much detail, from the dirty tank top, the ripped bra, and the poorly drawn eyeliner that one had to forget these details to arrive at a more general presentation. To use the taxonomic category, one had to discern Cherry's genus before one could ever hope to ascertain her species. She was that intricate. At her core, she was an enigma. Her scent was a blend of sweat, musk, and powder. It reminded me of a drugstore perfume that I had once smelled. It reminded me of the scent of Mallory's skin, the *Demeter Kitten Fur* that she had once sprayed when we were teenagers. Mallory had just died. Was I hallucinating her scent on this patient?

I greeted her with a neutral nonchalant, "Hi, Ms. Cherry. My name is Morgan Duchene. I'm a junior ER resident here. I'm here to evaluate you." Because I didn't know her last name, I decided to use her given name as a surname to appear more professional. She turned her head for a moment to look at me. But then she went into a corpse pose, reposing silently on the gurney. It appeared that she wasn't interested in what I had to say or do. However, a few seconds later she said, "I'm bleeding from my vagina. Please help me." She then touched her genitals and showed me a sliver of blood, as if she were telling me the truth, a way to validate her statement. "Oh, no, I understand, Ms. Cherry, that's why you're here. We'll figure this all out and stop the bleeding. But you must cooperate first. I need to gather a bit of history because that's very important in this case. Your blood pressure is a bit elevated, which, in this case, is a good sign. However, it's unexpected in this circumstance because you've been bleeding. Let me ask you some questions first, though."

I thought about my medical school years when we were introduced to simulated patients who were actors. This was done so we could understand the presentation of patients with various diagnoses and hone our medical acumen and bedside manner. I momentarily thought that Cherry was such a patient. She was so unlike anyone I had seen recently. But medical school and exams were over. This was real. Perhaps Death was testing me. There was nothing that fucker wouldn't try.

But, before I could say more, Cherry motioned me away, as if my monologue was pointless and boring her. "I'm tired. Let me sleep," she said softly, as if she had spent everything she had on this one brief statement. Lying there disheveled and dirty, Cherry appeared so desperate, so pure, so helpless, so lost. She looked like an injured animal that has no recourse but to yelp until someone helps it, like a wild baby deer that has been hit on the side of the door and left there. Her big black eyes pierced you, as if she could peer into your secrets. I looked away. She looked beautiful, too, in a very rugged way. There was no anger or resentment on her face, but there was pain, a great deal of pain. She was so tired of it all. I could sense that in her demeanor. She knew I could sense it, too. She had taken pain medications. She was clutching a small plastic bottle of Percocet, as if this one thing alone could provide her with that much needed solace. But both she and I knew that this would not provide any lasting comfort.

She needed love, for her loneliness, for her desperation, for herself. But there was no anger. There were just pills for the pain. She needed the universe to open its arms and bring her close to it, so she could experience its enormous warmth and companionship. Cherry had been wasted. She needed redemption, so she could go on living. She recognized that she would be wasted, again and again, if no one attempted a rescue. This was her last chance. With every minute, the chance of survival would diminish exponentially until she ceased to exist. But, to her, this was all pointless because she had fathomed that no one and nothing could save her. She had learned life's lesson all too brutally and all too wisely.

Cherry now knew that she had no chance in hell to survive in this world that cared nothing for people like her. She had given up. She would be all right with my friend, Death, that was all too eager to take her far, far away from her solitude and despair. No doubt, Death would then dispense her in a black hole. At that instant, I could see my dead sister lying there, and, in fact, wondered if Mallory had not really returned as Cherry to offer me a formal goodbye. I cried for Mallory. I cried for Cherry, too. I cried for them both, as I looked at this patient who looked so helpless and pure.

CHERRY

Cherry was wheeled into the emergency room of Massachusetts Hospital through two sets of double glass doors. The nurses parked her in a small space marked trauma 2 because, frankly, they didn't know what to do with her. She was bleeding profusely, but her blood pressure was increasing. They couldn't make sense of that, so she was placed in that space until an ER physician could evaluate her. Orders were placed for a variety of labs, including a complete blood count, metabolic panel, and a toxicology screen. Everyone was sure this was a case of drug abuse—perhaps PCP or Ecstasy/Molly or whatever the kids called it these days—because the presentation of the patient was so strange. However, what couldn't be readily explained was the hemorrhaging. Was this fibroids, or was this something more ominous, like gynecological cancer? But nothing seemed normal about this presentation.

A continuous blood pressure cuff was placed on Cherry's left forearm. A pulse oximeter was placed on the tip of the second digit of her right hand. Cherry did not complain or seem to register what was happening. She was like a rag doll, a catatonic individual, who would allow anyone to mold her as they wanted. She seemed to be extremely cold, so some flimsy white sheets were placed to warm her shivering body. The sheets turned crimson within a few minutes, as she continued to hemorrhage.

Approximately ten minutes later, the monitor would

alarm the nursing and medical staff that Cherry's blood pressure was plummeting. One minute after that, the pulse oximeter would reveal that her oxygen saturation was plunging. During that time, she would respond to questions posed to her with only brief and incoherent utterances. Several minutes later, she would be hyperventilating, taking shallow, rapid breaths. She would be administered Versed and Ativan to sedate her. She would be offered lidocaine and Bretylium to quell her aberrant heartbeat. Ultimately, she would be intubated and placed on a respirator. This would be the sequence of events that would befall Cherry in the emergency department at Massachusetts Hospital on June 11, 1996.

Code blue was announced on the hospital's speaker to announce that Cherry was undergoing a cardiopulmonary arrest. The code team rushed in the space behind the curtains to begin immediate resuscitative efforts. Defibrillator pads were attached to her chest. Paddles were pressed very firmly on her torso. Electrical contact was made with her smooth skin. Voltage was administered at 200 volts and increased by that amount every few minutes until Cherry's ventricular tachycardia had normalized to a sinus rhythm.

It was during those resuscitative efforts that the doctors and nurses would notice an oily sheen covering Cherry's body, as if she had just been immersed in an oil bath, as if her body were laminated with plastic. It was also during those efforts, when the doctors were intubating her, that they would smell a fruity, garlic-like odor arising from her mouth. The co-occurrence of these two unusual findings during a cardiac resuscitation was simply too much for everyone. The nurses and doctors were at a loss about this patient while trying to save her life in any manner they could. Cherry's torn bra was now lying on the floor of the cubicle, the bra that now not only smelled of sweat and sadness, but also of the blood and dirt of the hospital floor.

After Cherry's successful resuscitation, one of the nurses attempted to draw blood from her right arm. The nurse inserted a catheter and attached a syringe. As the syringe filled, the nurse was amazed and bewildered at what she smelled. An ammonia-like odor emanated from the tube. She leaned closer to the dying patient to trace the odor's source. A few weeks later, during the investigation of this case, she would say that she thought "Cherry's blood smelled like chemotherapy, the way blood smells putrid when people are taking some of those drugs. You know what I'm talking about, right?" At the smell, the nurse gagged and excused herself. A few minutes later, she was at the toilet vomiting vehemently, until nothing was left in her stomach. She then fainted.

Prior to heading for the bathroom, the nurse had handed the tube to the junior resident on call that night, Morgan Duchene. Morgan looked at the tube incredulously. Was this the patient's blood? she thought to herself. There were manila-colored particles floating in the blood, which normally should be pure and crimson. Instead, now, the blood had particles in it. She couldn't believe her eyes. She was feeling so nauseated and lightheaded. She also felt her face burning, like she imagined her deceased sister Mallory had felt when she had burned in the conflagration that killed her. Morgan excused herself from the trauma room and sat at a nurse's desk. Shortly thereafter, she fainted. A respiratory therapist who was also assisting in Cherry's resuscitation was the third person to pass out. She passed out on Cherry's dirty blood-and-dirt-soaked bra and vomited.

CHERRY

Besides having had to resuscitate Cherry, who was now in stable condition, the doctors in the ER had to care for the three women who had passed out from the patient's blood and bodily smell. The nurse and respiratory therapist both regained consciousness after several minutes but were confused. They still smelled that putrid and unusual odor that was wafting to the spaces nearby, but they seemed to be slowly regaining their senses. Contrary to science, could the patient's body be releasing toxic fumes, they thought?

Morgan Duchene had briefly lost consciousness at the nurse's station but was now awake and alert. She couldn't believe what had occurred to her. Never had she involuntarily lost her will and awareness. Never had she felt so powerless. She shivered for a few minutes while looking around her. Everything appeared to look the same but, in just a few minutes, her perception of the hospital had changed. She felt like she was on the set of a film production, as a clueless background actor who didn't know where she should stand or what she should do. There was no director to instruct her. The nurses and patients were staring at her, and she couldn't respond. "Doctor Duchene, are you alright?" they kept repeating. "Doctor Duchene, let's get you some electrolytes. It looks like you fainted." She felt stupid, but she finally arose and told everyone that she was fine, although she knew that she was anything but. What had hit her so forcefully and resulted in her fainting?

She vaguely remembered it now. It was the blood of the patient they were resuscitating. It was the manila-colored particles within that blood that had made her nauseous, like something she had seen in the film *Alien*, like an object that she couldn't register in her mind yet. Also, the oily sheen on Cherry's body and the garlic smell from her mouth had probably contributed to her nausea and fainting. What were those globules in the blood? She had never seen anything like it. An hour ago, Morgan had seen her sister in the final throes of life and pronounced dead, and now this. She couldn't reconcile the two episodes that were so unusual and dramatic. Could the two be somehow related?

Meanwhile, because the noxious odor from Cherry's room was being transmitted to other nearby spaces and given that three people had already fainted, the hospital administrators declared an internal emergency. An administrator and four clerks—all women—had also developed shortness of breath. As a result, other patients were taken outside, to the parking lot, to be evaluated. Some of the patients were nauseated and a few had vomited. However, no one else had fainted.

Under the dull orange glow of the parking lot's sulfur lamps, these patients were triaged. They were stripped down to their underwear. Their clothes were bundled into plastic bags, as if these articles were contagious. It was a scene outside: people undressing, people lying on the concrete ground, people controlling their urge to vomit. Inside the ER, the only people were the staff assisting Cherry, these being a vocational nurse, a respiratory therapist, and two physicians—Morgan Duchene and Stephen Adler, the chief resident.

Morgan attempted to stand but realized that she couldn't. She was now experiencing vertigo, along with her lightheadedness. Her eyes were becoming blurry and she couldn't see anyone distinctly. She called out to Stephen for some assistance, and, by that time, the chief resident knew that there was something distinctly wrong with Morgan. He attempted to conduct a neurological examination on Morgan, but before he could, she flailed her limbs, bit her tongue, and began convulsing.

It was during this commotion that the hazmat team entered the double glass doors of the ER. The team of two women and three men was bent on finding the origins and etiology of the volatile toxicant that could be lurking in the space within. The team searched for a variety of noxious chemicals that could cause such a scene. One culprit was hydrogen sulfide, an insidious poison that at high concentrations could cause death after several whiffs. The other contender was phosphine that could be used, on the one hand, for the preparation of various organic chemicals and, on the other, for chemical warfare—tearing capillaries in lungs and drowning victims in their own blood. None of these chemicals was detected, which, for the hospital staff, was a propitious sign. But the question remained: What was this unknown chemical?

MASSACHUSETTS DEPARTMENT OF
HEALTH & HUMAN SERVICES
INTERVIEW WITH LUCRETIA OWENS

Dr. Lina Anderson: Thanks for coming in, Ms. Owens. My name is Lina Anderson and I'm the director of Massachusetts Department of Health & Human Services. We're interviewing some of the staff who were in the ER the night of June 11, 1996, when Cherry presented there.

Lucretia Owens: (in a matter-of-fact manner): O.K.

Anderson: What was your role that night?

Owens: Like it always is. I was the head nurse who assisted in the intubation and resuscitation of Cherry. I was also the person who inserted the catheter to draw her blood.

Anderson: Yes, let's talk about the blood. Was there something unusual about it?

Owens: As I was inserting the catheter to draw the blood, the blood became solid and some particles formed in it. It smelled like chemotherapy, the way blood smells putrid when people are taking some of those drugs. You know what I'm talking about, right?

Anderson: I'm not a phlebotomist or nurse, but I think I know what you're getting at. Was there also something unusual about the patient's skin?

Owens: Yes. It had an oily sheen to it, sort of like someone had sprayed oil on her. The light was a little dim in the trauma space, but you could see that her skin was bright.

Anderson: How about her breath? Others in the ER have said that it smelled like garlic. Did you smell that odor on the patient?

Owens: Not at first. But when we started the resuscitation with the defibrillator, the odor just wafted throughout the ER. It smelled like ammonia. That's when I became nauseous and fell to the floor. I apparently lost consciousness for a few minutes.

Anderson: Did you notice anything about the IV bag that was connected to Cherry?

Owens: It looked a little bit more yellow than usual, but it wasn't anything out of the ordinary. Extra niacin usually makes the bags—banana bags, as we call them—yellow, so it was probably just that. Why are you asking?

Anderson: Well, there's a theory that that particular IV bag had methylamine in it with some nicotinamide. Basically, it is a precursor to methamphetamine. It's mixed with nicotinamide to add to the euphoria of meth. We're still working on that theory, though.

Owens: I don't know anything about that. Are we done here?

Anderson: Yes. If we have any more questions, we'll contact you. Here's my card if you remember anything else about that night.

Owens: O.K.

CHERRY

Incredibly, during this turmoil and lack of resources and personnel, both Cherry and Morgan were able to be stabilized. Cherry had just undergone a successful cardiac resuscitation. Morgan had sustained a seizure that had lasted several minutes. She then had a flurry of them for which she had to be intubated. She was stable but still unconscious. The two women were transported to the ICU for more studies and closer supervision.

Morgan was placed on a respirator. None of the physicians in this case entertained a viable diagnosis. They were at a loss for it. Was this infectious, given the strange characteristics of Cherry's blood? Was this, perhaps, a toxic reaction that had produced a byproduct they could not detect? Nothing made sense here. Nothing accorded with science. Morgan was placed in a medically induced coma, so her brain could be allowed to rest.

Cherry's hemorrhaging had also stabilized, but she, too, was unconscious. A sample of cells was taken were from cervix, which showed that she had stage IV cervical cancer. An MRI of her head further revealed that her cancer had metastasized to her brain, which could explain her confusion. Her diagnosis was grim.

They were placed in adjoining rooms. Curtains were drawn in both spaces. Cherry's room was restricted to scientists and physicians. Hazmat suits and corresponding masks were needed to enter her room. The smell of the ammonia and garlic, as well as the sheen on her skin, had partially resolved. She looked like a large, plastic doll, glistening somewhat, but not moving. She looked like death if no one knew better.

Morgan was in a better state. Although unconscious now, she had not sustained any lasting damage. The etiology of the seizures was concerning, but they were attributed to the noxious chemicals. An MRI of her brain was normal. She would briefly open her eyes and see the flickering lights in the ceiling. Then she would close them. During the times she was conscious, she felt exhausted and the memories of her fainting, the memories of Cherry's blood came rushing back to her. Then she would drift slowly back to sleep again. At times, the hospital staff would see Morgan speaking to herself, mentioning Cherry. They assumed she was hallucinating from the morphine that was being administered to her for the pain.

Cherry and Morgan. They were from a different time, but they were the same. Their meeting had been both a chance and an intended encounter. Could they have escaped their destinies? Would they be who they were destined to be despite altering the decisions that brought them here?

MASSACHUSETTS DEPARTMENT OF
HEALTH & HUMAN SERVICES
INTERVIEW WITH RUBY MAE O'HARA

Dr. Lina Anderson: Thanks for meeting with me, Ms. O'Hara. I hear that you've recovered now and feeling better. As you know, the Massachusetts Department of Health & Human Services, of which I'm the director, is interviewing certain individuals to better understand what happened to them on June 11, 1996, the date when Cherry presented to the ER. Now, can you tell me what happened to *you* that day?

Ms. Ruby Mae O'Hara: Well, first, I'm not completely better. I don't necessarily like it when people assume I am. This whole thing was so strange. I've never experienced anything like it. You know, I've been doing my job as an ER clerk for about thirty years now and haven't seen anything like this before. My grandson who's in Georgia, my hometown, always tells me, "Grandma, you need to..."

Anderson: Sorry to interrupt you, but if can you just answer the question, that'd be great. We don't have a lot of time here and this is an urgent matter. Again, can you please tell me what happened to you on that date?

O'Hara: I was getting to it before you so rudely interrupted me!

Anderson: I didn't mean to be rude but go on.

O'Hara: Cherry, that was the patient's name. She came in to register at the ER. She told me she was bleeding. She then stuck her hand in her private parts (ahem) and showed me blood. I almost gasped. Who does that? Not a proper lady, if you ask me. I thought she was just crazy. And the way she looked? As my co-workers say, girlfriend could've used some new clothes and a new hairdo. Whatever she did with herself was not working.

Anderson: Ms. O'Hara, let's just stick to the question. What happened before you passed out?

O'Hara: If that's what you really want. I was just trying to give you more information.

Anderson: I appreciate that, but let's get to the story.

O'Hara: I had taken Cherry's vitals and noticed a strange garlicky smell coming from her. At first, I thought that she had gone to an Italian restaurant and had too much garlic. You know, those bad Italian restaurants with lousy food where the cook puts garlic in everything to mask the taste. But then, I smelled it on her skin and everywhere. I became nauseated, you know? I almost gagged but then sent her to the head nurse. Her skin also looked a little greasy, like she'd put some Vaseline or some oil on it. It could've used a bit of cleaning. She looked so dirty and unkempt. Something just didn't seem right with her. Poor girl or I should say woman. I think she was younger than she looked, and she didn't look good.

Anderson: Now, this is an important question. Did her skin, as you put it, look oily to you then or was this afterwards when you saw her being intubated?

O'Hara: She absolutely looked that oily when I first saw her, and she smelled garlicky, too. I told you that already!

Anderson: I understand, but some of your colleagues think that Cherry presented to the ER, bleeding, but then, later, they noticed her skin and her strange odor when they were resuscitating her.

O'Hara: Well, I'm a keen observer of patients. That's my job. And I won't forget her face or smell. Ever. It's etched in my brain. Are you calling me a liar?

Anderson: Of course not. Just trying to get at the truth here. We're getting different accounts of the patient and they don't necessarily add up.

O'Hara: Uh huh.

Anderson: Well, let's continue. What about your passing out? Tell me about that.

O'Hara: Well, I was getting to that, if you'd give me a minute. So, an hour later, I went to ask Cherry some questions, to get her enrolled in Medicaid. She said she had no money to pay for the visit and she looked like she had just come from the streets, if you know what I mean (ahem). Well, I went to trauma 2, that's the space in the ER where we keep the more serious patients, and was surprised to see her intubated and in cardiac arrest. That surprised me so much! I mean, she was bleeding and all when she came in, but I didn't know it was that serious. I'm glad she was triaged to the trauma room.

Anderson: Continue, please.

O'Hara: Well, then that garlicky smell was all over the ER. I became even more nauseous and felt my blood pressure falling. Before I knew it, I passed out for a few minutes. I didn't know what had happened to me, but, afterwards, a few of the other nurses told me that I suddenly lost consciousness. I didn't feel anything before I passed out, but then I opened my eyes and there I was, in the ER again. That was so scary, child!

Anderson: I imagine it would be. Before you lost consciousness, did you see other people pass out, too?

O'Hara: Well, yeah, some of the nursing staff did and I think one of the junior residents in the ER did, too. Her name is Dr. Morgan Duchene. I don't mess with her. She's not very nice to us staff and she looks like a punk rocker, if you ask me, with her jet-black hair and nose ring. She's so rude. I'm not saying she deserved it, but it's probably good for her.

Anderson: Good for her?

O'Hara: Well, I just meant that she should experience a bit of hardship now and then. Missy thinks she knows everything, and she doesn't! She's such a smart ass, that Morgan, I mean Dr. Duchene.

Anderson: I think we're getting off track a bit. You were saying that you saw others passing out and then you passed out. Correct?

O'Hara: Right.

Anderson: Do you have a history of anxiety disorder, depression, or other psychological issues? I think your medical file mentioned that.

O'Hara: Are you calling me crazy? Well, I never…Wait. Who gave you access to my medical file, anyway? That's against HIPAA. You know, the medical privacy act, so no one snoops around your private information.

Anderson: Yes, I'm aware of HIPAA. You signed a waiver prior to this interview and gave us access to your medical records. Here you go. (She presents a consent form that O'Hara signed.)

O'Hara: I didn't know what that was. But, yes, I see a psychologist now and then, and take a medication for anxiety. It's not a big deal at all! The ER is not an easy place to work, with all these patients coming in and telling me about their problems. It gets me so tired and anxious. But let me see if I got this right. You're implying that I passed out because I saw other women doing it. Is that what you're saying? That's absurd.

Anderson: I didn't quite say that. But I think you just did.

O'Hara: You know, I don't like the tone of your voice. I know you're a director and all, but you've been curt with me during this interview. I'm doing you a favor here. I'm also not crazy because I think you were going down that road. I'd like to stop this interview, thank you very much!

Anderson: All right. If that's how you feel. Thanks for your time.

Part III
FATIMA

I find myself at the psychiatric ward at Massachusetts Hospital. I'm lying on a bed. I've been involuntarily taken here. I see woman of all ages around me, but mainly young ones. Why have they taken me to this facility? Why have they sequestered me here? What do they hope to do with me? What are their intentions? I have so many questions but no answers. I remain awake and then my head nods off, and I'm back to sleep. I sleep for mere seconds and then I awaken. I often lose consciousness. The women look at me. Some have distorted faces. Some have faces that do not move. They remain there. Who are they? Why are they so strange? I see movement. Some jerk their bodies, hips thrusting, as if they were copulating. Some seem to smile at me while doing this. Is this a show? Are they putting a show on for me? They get a lot of attention, these women who thrust and gyrate their bodies. The doctors call them hysterics. The doctors call them incurables. They try to see what makes these women move and gyrate. They try to see what makes them expel white foam and drool from their mouths. Whatever it is, these doctors consider it a disease of women. But why am I here? I do not move like they do. I do not look like they do. In fact, this frenzied and ritualized madness frightens me. No, I'm not one of them. Can't the doctors see this? I do not belong in this asylum of crazies.

As I was drifting to sleep tonight, I felt that someone had restrained and gagged me. I felt a large wet rag in my mouth. I couldn't scream. I wanted to scream so forcefully and shatter the windows of this asylum, this prison, but I couldn't. I couldn't even move, couldn't flinch a muscle, although I was fully conscious and awake. And then I saw a black monster hover above me. Its eyes were fiery red. It had horns. It protruded its long, red tongue, and aimed for my face. Then it came and sat on me. It wouldn't allow me to breathe. It was suffocating me, squeezing me so tightly. I felt this pressure would soon release my soul. And then I saw several black skulls floating above me. They were making their way toward me. They were skulls of heads, detached from their bodies. They had such large teeth. Hunger was in their eyes. They were so hungry for me. I could see that. But I couldn't scream. I couldn't move to strike them. I have never felt such horrors. And that's when I saw that the black monster, looking like a vivid gargoyle now, take me in its arms. It flew me to the ceiling. It attempted to drop me on the floor. I was like glass, so fragile and cold. But then I suddenly could move again. I realized that I was grounded, in my own bed. What horrors are these? Am I mad? Do I really belong in this asylum of mad women? They can tell me what they want, but I know that I was not dreaming this.

They call him Dr. Deutermann, he who visits us in the morning. He is a heavy man. His face is round and large. His hair is ghastly white and thinning. His forehead is large and oily. Although he hasn't spoken to me yet, I already detest him and loathe anything connected to him. I detest this hospital. This Deutermann is not satisfied until he sees the women dancing and thrusting for him. The women are perfectly normal until he walks into the room and, then, they start at it. What a spectacle! They all vie for his attention. Each wants to outdo the other in this macabre, epileptic dance. I don't understand them. After the dance, this Deutermann measures their secretions and their hysterical moisture. That's what he calls it. It's a disgusting sight, as if they're animals to be selected and bred. Are these women so desperate for attention that they're willing to confine themselves to this hospital? Where do I fit into this? I do not know this yet. I'm afraid that my role in all of this and my fate are even more devastating than I initially thought. Deutermann looks at me more and more every day. He doesn't say a word. He knows that I won't perform for him, like the others. He walks past my bed. He offers me a sideways glance, making sure that I see him see me. Yet, he won't speak. I don't wish to speak to him, either. I'm convinced this is all a game and I'm a pawn in this.

He comes closer and closer to me, this Deutermann, without saying a word. I smell his rancid sweat and antiquated breath. I feel his filthiness on my neck. He has not showered for quite some time. He sniffs me, each time he inches towards me, as if I'm tender morsel. His nose is beaked and sharp. At times, I believe that he is a bald eagle, coming to capture me with his sharp talons. He looks like an eagle. I feel that he will one day use his sharp beak and carry me, his prey, away with his talons. I truly detest him. He may be strong. However, I'm faster than he is. He walks slowly, so very slowly. His protuberant belly slows him down. In some ways, however, I'm so much weaker than he is. I experience throbbing headaches daily. I faint and lose control. I don't know the cause for this. My mother thought I had been infused by the evil loa, Maman Brigitte. In Haitian voodoo, she is the loa associated with the death and the underworld. She is the icy finger of death, of mortality. To ward off this spirit, my mother gifted me with a necklace made of magical herbs, of dragon blood resin, vetivert, and agrimony. My father, a devoted Muslim, thought jinn and the evil eye had overwhelmed me. He gave me an evil eye pendant to bounce the hex to its sender. The jinn hide everywhere, he told me, in rats, dogs, snakes, and even in shadows. None of these amulets worked to cure me. They took them away when I came here.

Today, for the first time, Deutermann addressed me. With a strong and forceful German accent, as if he were hiding the fact that he was anything other than German, he said, "So, your name is Fatima? I'm assuming you're of African origin. The color of your skin gives you away. Your scent doesn't help, either. I smell your origin." I remained paralyzed for a few seconds and didn't say anything. I hoped he would think that I only spoke the African language. He continued. "I have a guest who will be coming to this ward. He will try to cure you. I can't do much with you. You're worthless to me." I didn't respond this second time, either. He walked away, languidly, giving me a quick glance.

In the Arabic language, Fatima means to abstain. Before I was brought here unwillingly, I thought I knew how to abstain, to rein in my impulses. But I've had enough of this. At that moment, all I could feel in this psychiatric asylum, with Deutermann looking at me and smelling me like some sort of prey and animal, was hate, true and utter hate. How I wished he were dead. How I wish I was the one who would kill him while he slept. I wouldn't abstain.

I know that I'm not the only one who saw this. Perhaps, I'm the only one who's consciously aware of it. Or the only one who cares. Today, Deutermann, with his wide girth and heavy stance, came to the bed of a girl, Millie. She is the same age as I am: eighteen, as she later told me. He placed his right hand upon her genitals. It was then that Millie gave out a piercing cry. She began convulsing. I was perhaps twenty feet from her, so I couldn't see her too well. But Millie would convulse and freeze. This continued for a few minutes. She then seemed to lose all energy. Deutermann then lifted and carried her away to an adjacent room. I don't know the purpose of that room. I certainly wouldn't want to be taken there. As Deutermann lifted Millie, I saw that he touched her groin. He began caressing that area. He kept rubbing and rubbing her genitals. Does he want her to convulse again? Is this a sort of desire for her? This Deutermann is filthy. You can tell by his soiled, white jacket. I have my eyes on him. But I don't think this will end well for poor Millie.

That night, I dreamt in red. Red was at the heart of my dream. It was everywhere. Red. I couldn't make out anything else. Everything had blended into it. Like a Red curtain that has been suddenly opened, I saw a theater of beasts being killed. It was a slaughterhouse. Blood then started flowing again. It filled up that entire space. Millie then appeared. Her blonde hair had turned crimson. Blood was dripping from her forehead. She was being nailed. She was being crucified on a wooden cross. All the while, she kept looking at me, with an intense gaze, as if to say, you did nothing for me when I was taken to that back room. She continuously screamed, but I couldn't hear anything. It was a silent scream. Millie was twisting herself in all directions. She was like a worm that has been pinned and is trying to escape. She writhed. Her spasms were chaotic. I ran to her. I attempted to pry her off that cross. That's when she bit me. She started to devour me. With unrestrained energy and rigor, she took out the nails herself and threw herself at me. She chewed my flesh. She had a large grin, as if she were finally given what she had desired. Her voice was now audible, but it was gibberish to me. She then devoured me with her entire mouth, in one gulp. I then vanished into her. I awoke, my heart beating like a horse's. I had wetted the sheets with my urine. I was sweating profusely, like a pig.

Millie. She remains immobile and stares at the wall. She doesn't convulse any more, even when Deutermann walks besides her bed. Her hysterical antics have disappeared. Deutermann doesn't even lift her up to caress her legs and genitals. You can see that he's disgusted with her now. How cruel and despicable this Deutermann is. Millie looks dead, except she still has a pulse and breathes. Deutermann confirms this, but that's it. No more deep caresses from him. He is now eyeing me more and more each day. Am I to be his next conquest? The other women in the room remain just as mute as Millie. They still dance their epileptic dances, perhaps hoping that Deutermann will take them to the back room. They're hoping to be selected by the most powerful man at Massachusetts Hospital. But they're so gullible! They'll be tossed away in the rubbish like the rest of them. I won't let this happen to me.

Deutermann's friend has come to visit the hospital. They call him Henry Sullivan. Unlike Deutermann, he has dark curly hair. He is of Irish descent. He looks kind. His eyes are warm. He also carries a heavy beard. His mustache is manly and curled at the ends. He looks like a God-man, what I imagine Allah to look like. Both kind and stern, but also powerful. I don't dislike him. He is quiet. He doesn't say much. He walks slowly behind Deutermann. He observes what that despicable man does. Sullivan is intelligent but doesn't make a spectacle of it, unlike that obese old man. He simply observes, while Deutermann gesticulates like a monkey. I detest Deutermann more so because of what he did to that young girl. Poor Millie. Deutermann has told this Sullivan something. Sullivan looks at me. He quickly looks away. He's shy. I don't know what they're talking about. I'm certain that it's about my illness. After all, that's why I'm here. Or so I think. They've made their way toward me. Deutermann tells Sullivan that he can't quite figure out my illness. I'm not hysterical like the other women. I'm still yet a puzzle, an enigma of sorts. He tells Sullivan that I have difficulty speaking. He tells him that I have weakness of my face and limbs. He tells him that I have blurred vision. He tells him that I have headaches, that I lose consciousness. They can't quite figure this out, the dynamic duo. I'm not like the other women here. I'm special. What will become of me here?

Today marks my fourth month in this psychiatric ward. I have grown accustomed to this place. I know that I won't be going anywhere. I will die here. Sullivan's fingernails are now always coated with a white substance. Cocaine. He is invigorated whenever he takes a hit. He's addicted to this. At times, he lashes out at me, not physically, but verbally. "Fatima, why don't you give up this charade, this performance?" he says, striking the wall. But, mostly, he's kind and tender, as soft as a teddy bear. He's addicted to me. I'm merely a specimen, an experiment for him, for them. Sullivan keeps a notebook on me. He measures my pupils before and after. He checks to see how long my symptoms have lasted. I believe that I lost consciousness again today, that I had difficulty speaking. But I'm not sure anymore. He measures my cervix. He measures my milky secretions. He measures my sex. And then he lifts me and takes me to my bed. He kisses me on the forehead, as I then go to sleep. Do I empathize with him? Empathize that he's also part of this circus over which he has little control? He's being manipulated by that pig, that despicable Deutermann. That much is clear.

They have brought a new girl into our already crowded and despicable quarters. Her name is Sylvia. Her hair is long and wispy blonde. It appears that she may have wanted to cut it. She was unsuccessful. Sylvia's expression is stern. She has the look of the devil about her. She curses so much, as if she wants to destroy this place and everything that goes with it. She is determined to be a rebel and usurp Deutermann's position in this facility. She urinates so much. Her blood is often mixed with her foul urine. But Deutermann gathers the urine into a cup and measures it. He dissolves a salt into the cup. He watches it foam. He makes some calculations of her sex and then moves on. Sylvia attempts to batter Deutermann and claw him with her long fingernails while he and Sullivan make their rounds. She is slow. He is faster and moves on. I see him grinning. He knows that he still holds power over all of us. This Sylvia. So, she, too, is powerless against the madness of this asylum. So, she, too, will rot away like I will. I see her future so clearly now.

Today is a strange day. I see a man hovering over me. He's neither Deutermann nor Sullivan. He wears a hat. He has a small build. He's short. He holds a finger to his nose. He whispers "Shh!" Who is he? He says he's Millie, dressed as a man. So, it is Millie! What is she doing? She tells me that she plans to escape from his asylum. She has had enough of this circus, of this debauchery. If she should die during this escape, so be it. She says that she's already dead anyway. They can't kill her twice. I look at her. What gentle features. Won't they see through her? How can she manage to escape? Why has she confided in me? She says that I'm the smart one. The others are worthless mutes to her. They won't say anything. They can't think anymore. But I'm different. So how I am to help her? She tells me that I should start convulsing, that I should create a spectacle, so as to distract them. I'm so special, she tells me, that the doctors will all flee to me. They will see this extraordinary show of hysteria. I have seen enough of this spectacle to do as Millie says. But part of me wants her here. Part of me wants her caught. Part of me wants her dead. Why give her the opportunity to escape, while I remain here? She then tells me that if she escapes, she will see to it that I also leave this despicable place. Do I believe her? I have no other choice. She is my only hope of an escape. I must trust her. I must see this through and see how it plays out.

Millie fled down the staircase and out of this insane asylum. She was successful! She came through the front door of this asylum as a woman. She left as a man. She opened the door and left. I'm dumbfounded. Her ruse worked. When she prompted me, I started convulsing, like no one ever has. It was so believable, so genuine. Even the other women in the room were in awe. I thrust my hips, flailed my limbs, and urinated. I even bit my tongue with the hot, red blood flowing from my mouth. I can still taste that acidity. I have to admit, it was the best performance here. The other doctors instantaneously notified Deutermann and Sullivan. They came running to me in no time. Everyone gathered around me, as if this were an extraordinary event, one that would occur only once in a lifetime. The commotion was staggering. As the two doctors approached me, running, I felt that I should stop convulsing. They could see through this. I had already urinated and bit my tongue. That was enough for them, at least for today. Deutermann and Sullivan are now convinced they know what is ailing me. But this is for show, I wanted to say. This is not real. They looked to one another like they had solved a puzzle. But I wanted to say to that loser, Deutermann, who is the mastermind of this entire lunacy: Walk out, walk out, and take that obese, protuberant belly with you.

In this asylum, we are all night creatures. We lie in stealth. Our desires rouse us from a non-existence. Deutermann is the alpha male. Millie has fled from his clutches. But he was no longer interested in her. Once he possessed her, she no longer had him under her spell. She was useless to him. Sullivan follows in Deutermann's wake. He is a quieter night creature. He makes sure he is camouflaged before he strikes. His clutch is weaker, but his ambition is just as strong. He attempts to suppress his desire toward me, but he is weak for that. He wants. He gets. I, too, want. I, too, desire. But in this asylum of women, our desires do not matter. We are night creatures of a different sort. We are their prey. They feed upon us. We dig our boroughs, deep and deeper. We claw through the mud. We attempt an escape. Millie was the first of us to do it. In her wake, we may have a chance yet. Am I kidding myself? They'll tighten the reins even more. We'll suffocate. I thought I had a chance of escape. Now that chance has evaporated. Do I believe Millie when she says that she'll rescue me from their clutches, from this madhouse? I want to believe. Hope is all I have. I have traced my escape through the labyrinth of my mind. Each time, I manage to escape through the secret passageways. I can see them so vividly. I know the maze so well. But my mind is not an asylum. I know that. I practice and practice, so that my mind and the asylum converge. I will excavate deeper and deeper. I will not let them see me burrowing. You have underestimated me,

Deutermann and Sullivan. I will lie in wait. I will strike at the most opportune time. I will fight you through the end of days. You'll see. I will outwit the both of you at your own miserable game. I will leave. I will take my person with me, the only thing that I now possess.

The asylum is in a commotion today, but they won't tell us girls anything. Deutermann and Sullivan appear extremely distressed. Something of importance has happened here, but it's futile to inquire about this, especially after Millie's recent escape. Deutermann even yells at Sullivan. With his chatter, Deutermann's protuberant belly expands further. I'm slurring my words even more so today. I feel unbalanced when I attempt to walk. I haven't slept in days. My stomach also appears to be growing every day. I feel that I may be pregnant, although no one has confirmed this. All signs point to this. I'm no longer menstruating. I'm nauseous. My breasts have swollen. My brain is foggy. Sullivan makes his rounds and looks at my cervix. It's taken on a purple-red hue, he says. "We've also injected your urine into one of the mice here. The urine has produced a bulging mass on its ovary." He assuredly confirms my pregnancy, as if I'm some animal, but shows no emotion for his future child. What is to happen to this child I may be carrying? How will I treat this child of mine who will be born of disgust and revolt? I believe this has all been an experiment. They want to see what kind of child I will beget. Will this child have the same condition as I do? Will they finally get their answer through this experiment of theirs? What will become of me once I deliver? What will become of my child? The thinking is exhausting me. It's sapping me of necessary nutrients reserved for my bastard child. This is all I can muster today. I am becoming weaker, day by day.

My stomach is growing, as if someone is injecting it with water every day. My body is simply an aqueduct to convey necessary fluids to my bastard child. It's also a temporary home in which this child will reside until birth. Deutermann and Sullivan come around to see me every few weeks. They notice it all. They notice my protuberance. They notice my engorged breasts, my edematous legs and feet. They measure every inch of me, down to my vulva. I still don't know what they want from me. I recognize that this child is part of the answer. They don't need me anymore. They need my child. They're anticipating the birth, as if it will be a miracle. Deutermann and Sullivan don't talk to me. They simply glance at my body. This is the only thing that holds an answer for them. They look at my face with disgust. I only ask one thing of them. "If the child is a girl, please name her Nadia." My request catches them off guard. Sullivan's left eyebrow peaks. I then turn my back against them. I'm dead to them already. They've thrown me in the rubbish.

I feel myself rotting away. Slowly. That's the worst of it. I'm conscious of my body. I'm conscious of the strange things that are happening to it. Liquid is oozing from me. My organs are becoming simultaneously soft and hard. I can hardly think anymore. I involuntarily urinate all the time. And yet, there's no one here to help me through this. My stomach is obese. It is beyond recognition now. The other women notice. Deutermann and Sullivan decide to move me to that detested back room in the asylum. That is smart of them. After all, to whom do the other women think this child belongs? Am I like the Virgin Mary who has been inseminated despite no sexual intercourse? I'm dead to myself. I'm dead to others. Though this child that I'm carrying is a bastard and born in such vile circumstances, I owe it the gift of life. A life that will be already tainted, but, perhaps, which it can outgrow. I don't foresee that I'll have any part to play in this. Poor thing. This devil child will have to fend for itself.

How weak I've grown. I am growing weaker every day. I was wrong about the child. It's no good. The child is sapping everything that I've got. I'm afraid it will be the death of me. It's as if this pregnancy has been a way to get rid of me. It has been a devious plan concocted by Deutermann and Sullivan all along. The chemicals—progesterone and estrogen—swim inside me. They follow a pattern, a pattern of which I know so little. These compounds announce me on my person. It's as if my sex is written upon me, like some scarlet letter. Always, they target me. Always, they survey me. In my weakness and sleeplessness, however, I've grown so sexual. The doctors can smell me from such a distance! A mare in heat. I no longer care for this little vampire inside me that is sucking me of nutrients and blood. Sucking a little everyday but sucking me to death, nonetheless. This little, baby vampire.

It won't be long now. They tell me that. To my horror, the belly will momentarily give way to a bastard child. Deutermann and Sullivan have told me so. How excited they are! What are they planning to do with this child? I'll let the fates decide her future. How are they planning to get rid of me? This is what frightens me the most. I remain in the back room. I'll soon be relieved from this child, from this body. It's certain. They've come. Sullivan approaches me. I see his full, brown beard, although I'm delirious. I see white powder deposited on his beard. He has sniffed another line. He has taken another hit of cocaine. He reeks of gin. His hair has grown abundantly. It looks wild. He measures my cervix. It has dilated more. It is expanding. It's so painful. I feel the devil's child throb against me, like a heart that's about to explode. The child's heart feels like a dagger. It tries to pierce and penetrate my belly. I feel myself in a sea of blackness. The sea is rough. I'm a ship that will soon crash against the rocks. I know that I'll soon see the face of Allah. I'll become the God-woman. Inshallah. I have suffered so much. This has to be! I will become his God-bride. I'm trying to avoid the rocks. I try to flow with the wave. I feel something stretched from me. I'm pushing so hard. I push and push. But I can't see a thing. I feel that something is about to leave my body. Sullivan tells me to push harder. In that moment, his face becomes almost heavenly and bright. I can't make out an outline. I hear trumpets. I hear a song of jubilee. I feel myself traversing dark corridors. I climb through a dark window. I see a heavenly child run down the corridor from which I've come. I tell her to stop. I'm her mother. But she keeps running. She suddenly looks back at me. She laughs. And then she looks worried for me. She comes running to me, frowning. But I'm somewhere else now. I'm lost. I'm swimming in a sea of blood. I'm climbing into the Tower of Hell. I smell smoke. I feel ashes against me. I hear the clanging of a bell. I see the face of Allah. I feel the beak of a large bird that devours me. I don't care at all. And at that instant, I am no more. I now know that I'm not the seed of Allah. I'm not the God-woman. I'm nothing.

Part IV
THE MAN
& NADIA

THE MAN

You will undoubtedly feel sorry for me as you get to know me. I'm a loser, both literally and figuratively. Since I can remember, I've lost but never found. I'm still looking. Professionally, I'm a highly respected chemist, for all that's worth. Though most do not know this, I'm also a paranormal investigator and an enthusiast in all things psychological. It's an interest I've had since I began my formal education in the chemical sciences. I don't usually relay this information because it makes me appear less empirical. It detracts from my accomplishments. But let's make this clear. I'm not a ghostbuster. I'm not a ghost hunter. I'm not a psychical researcher. Beyond everything, I'm a scientist who has interests in the paranormal. I can recite physics equations and theorems; I can regurgitate chemical nomenclatures and postulates; I can tell you how fast a nanoparticle can travel intercellularly or intracellularly; I can differentiate between quarks, protons, and neutrons. In short, I'm no quack. I may have an interest in the unknown and what science cannot ascertain, but I consider myself a scientist, first and foremost. In my opinion, the two are not mutually exclusive. Science and the paranormal can coexist and, in fact, they often do. I'm here to prove it.

I'm also not one to sugarcoat. I never was. I told the real estate agents exactly what I wanted in a home. I informed them that I wanted a house in which someone had died. But I also wanted a home to die in, more precisely, a place to kill myself. I omitted the last part, knowing full well that they wouldn't sell me a home if they knew my true intentions. Unlike other home buyers who never *truly* say what they *desire* in a house, though they know what they *want*, I knew exactly what I desired and needed. Death was my aim. Death was my trajectory. The house would merely be my destination, a receptacle to keep me reposed for eternity.

I don't think this was too unusual of a request. If I should die, should I not be allowed to select the place or the spirits with whom I'd live? You can call it a camaraderie of sorts, a guarantee that I wouldn't be alone in that house that I would inhabit for eternity. I wanted a ghost as a companion for life. I wanted a conversationalist. I didn't desire solitude. I didn't want to be dead alone. One death was good enough for me. One companion could satiate me for a lifetime, or so I thought.

Despite my best intentions and transparency, no one took the bait, as I had anticipated. As you can imagine, not only were the options and inventory for homes in Providence limited, but the agents themselves were not very accommodating. I don't blame them. They thought they were dealing with an absolute lunatic or pervert, at best. Despite the commission they would earn from the sale, most were unsurprisingly skeptical. It was the sixth agent who took me seriously when I named my requirement. Her name was Agnes Winterbottom.

Agnes had an authentic British London accent and didn't even wince at my request. We initially spoke on the phone. She answered on the first ring. I explained my dilemma. She responded without missing a beat and just continued talking: *Are you looking for a death in a particular year or century? I particularly think deaths in the nineteenth century are absolutely charming,* she said, her voice calm and collected. At that moment, I thought she could be crazier than I was and tried to gauge if she was the right agent for such a job. *And does this person have to be a certain gender or race, or have a certain sexual orientation? And, lastly, must the death have occurred naturally or by violent means? I think naturally is undoubtedly better, but I also particularly like a bit of intrigue, if you know what I mean. A warm gun or a poisoned laudanum concoction. Wouldn't that be absolutely grand?* I was flabbergasted, to say the least. *Now they don't make deaths like that anymore, do they?* she continued rambling. *These days, deaths are so shabby, unlike the glorious ones that we're used to. They are threadbare to the core? Am I right in my assessment, Mr....?* I bypassed her demand for a name and just began speaking. *I totally agree,* I said, a bit bemused but also relieved. Was she an Agatha Christie aficionado? I assumed she was. There was an intrigue in the way she described things, as if she was looking for something deeper than there actually was, a mystery that lurked behind everything, even the mundane. She said all these things casually, like she was selling me a suit at a department store. I didn't know if she was cajoling me to incriminate myself in some sort of crime that I may have committed or would commit. But she finally winked and smiled devilishly at me, as if she were an accomplice in my own game. I dismissed my theory.

I must admit that I was impressed by Agnes's response. She went on to say these things without a hint of intimidation, fear, or sarcasm. She had even thought about things that I had not deliberated or cared to think about. Her tone was affable and lighthearted despite my somber request. She took me at my word and didn't pry. After some inner reflection, I felt that I had found the right agent in Agnes. I was sure of this.

I met Agnes on an unusually cold, rainy day in June. It was the perfect weather for the house that I desired. She appeared just as I imagined her: a woman in her mid-50s of average height. Her hair was cast in a tightly wound bun and had turned partly grey at the edges. She hadn't even attempted to color it. *Good for you*, I wanted to say to her, but I thought this was not very appropriate when we had just met. She wore an old-school cardigan, which was properly buttoned. The cardigan was a bit tight for her, but it showed her large breasts off nicely. I don't know if that's the look she was going for, but it worked for her, quite well, I should add. Old-school charm with a bit of subtle sexiness was certainly refreshing in this college town with sweatshirts that announced RISD or Brown University without subtlety. That blatant show of Ivy League superiority was suffocating, to say the least, so Agnes's charm was doubly refreshing.

I was sort of attracted to Agnes but not in a way that you'd expect. She wasn't my type, but I admired her bravado. I must admit that she was way too good looking for me. You see, I'm not very attractive. My very elongated features and sunken eyes give me away as the freak I am.

I'm abnormally thin with disproportionately long arms, legs, and fingers. I have pockmarks on my cheeks, deep scars that I accumulated because of acne in my teenage years. It was during that time when I was diagnosed with Marfan syndrome, a genetic disorder that affects my connective tissues. I also have an abnormally curved spine and am extremely near-sighted. Without glasses, I can't see a thing, even my shoes. Perhaps, this is how I became a scientist and a paranormal enthusiast. As a child, I liked to remain alone. Kids at school looked at me like they would a monster. Instead of mocking me, as you'd expect, they were terrified of me. I towered above them and, although thin, had the advantage of my height during any combat. If you must know, I'm six feet six inches in height. I have a large forehead. I have a breastbone that protrudes outward, as if my chest is enormous. In short, I'm a regular Frankenstein's monster. People regard me suspiciously when they initially meet me. But not Agnes.

I met her on the outside stairs of the first house I saw and that I would eventually purchase. The house was nothing special. The exterior did not convey that there was anything worth looking at inside. The yard was unkempt, with overgrown shrubbery. Plants were wilting. There was a small garden alongside the home with weeds and wilting wildflowers. The chairs on the balcony had been there for ages, I surmised. The color of the home had taken on a sepia hue, like the photographs of the late 19th century. In short, although the house was not dilapidated, in the true sense of the word, it was in poor condition and slowly rotting away. It had the makings of a genuinely haunted house.

That is exactly what I needed. I desired a new beginning, in a college town, one that hearkened to the way I used to live in my early adulthood. I wanted to get away from myself and languish in a place that had little identity. In short, I wanted to kill myself and this was a perfect place to do so. Had I thought about committing suicide? Most assuredly. Had I really conceived a plan, though? Not yet anyway. Frankly, I had no energy. I couldn't think clearly. But I knew that I would do it soon, and in this house. It was really befitting me, this house on Angell Street, a Victorian, now covered in sepia haze, with wildflowers and shrubbery that hadn't been cut for months. It resembled my inner chaos. I was instantly attracted to it.

After our usual polite introductions, Agnes prodded me on. *Well, do you want to look inside?* she said. "The house hasn't been occupied for more than twenty-six years since its owner presumably died in 1970. I say presumably because rumor has it that she died here but her body subsequently disappeared. I can't attest to the validity of that, but be though as it may, rest assured that we are almost certain she died here. I think we can negotiate a very good deal with the agent." Agnes's tone was calm and collected. She didn't even comment on my appearance, nor did she seem awed by it. I was even more drawn to her. She was a gift and so was this decrepit house.

NADIA SULLIVAN,
ÉLAN VITAL:
A STUDY IN LIFE UNEXPLAINED (EXCERPTS)

The contents of this personal and short monograph, *ÉLAN VITAL: A Study in Life Unexplained*, allude to my professional and personal life experiences. As such, it can be considered a semi-autobiographical account, if you will. It is a journal of what I assume to be my last days on earth and my current reflections on the power of the mind, of the power of the unknown. I was hesitant to embark upon such a task because I felt it would detract from my work as a behavioral neuroscientist, insofar as this text delves into spirituality and religious studies, two disciplines that are in direct contrast with my specialty and focus. Nevertheless, based on my recent observations and tenuous grip on good health, I cannot continue to avoid these matters, as they have significance beyond my life and implications for others. In other words, I have decided to espouse a Kantian Duty Based, or Deontological, Ethics. I feel that I am morally obligated to act in accordance with a certain set of principles and rules regardless of outcome. Time is of the essence, given my ill health. As such, I cannot be derelict in my duties as a researcher and scientist, even if most of what I am to disclose is not empirically based. I may be ridiculed in the medical and scientific communities for this monograph, but I feel this disclosure is significantly more important than my reputation, be that as it may.

Recently, I have begun to understand the implications

that Buddhism has had on modern behavioral neuroscience and its role in memory and amnesia. This has had a profound impact on my life, as I will later discuss. Buddhism asks: Why are we suffering from amnesia of our spiritual origins? It offers four responses, which I think are highly valuable in this context, these being 1) one enters the fetus unaware and unknowing and is born with amnesia, 2) pre-birth memory is intact but is lost while in the womb and continues after birth, 3) pre-birth memory remains intact until birth trauma induces forgetfulness, and 4) pre-birth memory is intact, and one is born fully conscious of the Soul's journey. To my astute readers who have been following my work, this excursion from my previous texts may seem a bit too "unscientific" and untenable. Rest assured, I have grappled with these facts for quite some time, but at the present, I cannot, and will not, dismiss these theories as supernaturally preposterous. They have validity and profound implications for behavioral neuroscience.

Research into memory and birth trauma has revealed that during human birth, the baby and womb are bathed in oxytocin once contractions begin. Oxytocin is the mother's hormone for causing or strengthening uterine contractions during childbirth, as well as aiding in the flow of breast milk. As several researchers have opined, including one of my colleagues, Thomas Verny, MD, oxytocin accounts, in part, for the amnesia during birth.[2] To instill feelings of intimacy and to eliminate alienation, oxytocin allows the mother and baby (the former to a lesser extent) to

2   Thomas Verny, *The Secret Life of the Unborn Child*. New York: Dell, 1981.

forget birth trauma and induces feelings of trust and love. For this reason, it's often called the "love hormone." In animal studies, oxytocin induces a biochemical amnesia. This amnestic effect continues when a baby is breastfed, if sufficient oxytocin is available in the mother's milk.

You may ask why some individuals remember their time before birth and others don't. My recent interest and research into Greek philosophy answers this question to a certain extent. For example, in Plato's Myth of Er, incarnating Souls journey through a torrid region before reaching Lethe, the underworld river of oblivion. In this journey, the wise, or dry, Soul resists the elixir of amnesia and retains pre-birth memories. However, a wet Soul, who has drunk of the river, has so imbibed itself of the Lethean potion that it has no recollections of its past life. There are other versions of this concept in other cultures, such as in India, where sages affix retention of pre-birth memory to higher consciousness. But they all highlight the significance of a pre-birth memory that can remain pristine if certain guidelines are followed. Of course, the Soul's journey is complicated and may not be under one's volition.

Pythagoras of Samos, the ancient Ionian Greek philosopher, has outlined the process of a Soul's descent from the spiritual realm to earth. Initially, the Soul is overcome with heaviness, melancholy, and dread in having to leave divine life, although an invincible force also attracts it to earthly life. In the second phase, as heaviness increases, a dimness is felt wherein the Soul can only feebly see its spiritual companions. It hears their sad farewells.

It imagines their tears. But, alas, it's too late. It has left and is too far to return to its spiritual realm. However, the Soul promises to remember this delightful memory, as it descends in the dense atmosphere of Earth. Finally, during the Soul's descent, a guide points out its future mother, where the Soul then plunges into the womb and the memory of divine life is extinguished (with the exception of the dry Souls we previously discussed).

My theories of pre-life do not correspond to the elaborate scientific work that I had been previously conducting into the role of the hippocampus and temporal lobes of the brain and its connection to Alzheimer's disease. But that does not mean this current exposition is less relevant or exigent, as I will shortly expand on.

Agnes took out what looked like a skeleton key and began to open the door. As I mentioned, the door had taken on a brownish amber that was not attractive. It looked unpleasantly old and one that had not been maintained very well. There were some scratches on it, too. The thought of cougars clamoring to get into the home to kill their next victim forcefully intruded my thoughts. *Maybe that's how the victim or victims died*, I thought. I wouldn't broach the topic of the victim's death yet until I had seen the home. It would look very suspicious.

It took Agnes several attempts before I heard a click. *Here we go*, she said. *I haven't seen this home yet. Well, shall we take a look, Mr....?* Another attempt was made to decipher my name. I resisted it. Agnes, being totally professional, decided to let the question slide once more.

The door creaked, as if it hadn't been opened for years. Several seconds were needed before my pupils could accommodate the darkness that surrounded us. It was so very dark, with no lights whatsoever. A stale, yellow smell permeated the house. It was resonant of sadness, of inheritance gone awry. Agnes was nowhere to be found. I immediately thought that she had been a figment of my imagination, a hallucination that I had somehow conjured. She was too good to be true. I began waving my arms, so that I could touch her to know that she really existed, that our encounter was genuinely that fortuitous. Darkness is all that I could grab until I heard her proper British accent squirm out of that void. *Mr....are you alright? I was trying to find the switch to the light but then I fell. There is a step here. Be careful.* Her voice reverberated in this empty void. The hollowed space boomeranged our voices back to us. It was delightfully spooky, the way a theremin projects sound. If I hadn't been sold by the façade of the house, I was now. *I'm O.K., Ms. Winterbottom. I just can't see,* I responded. *Here, give me your hand.* Our echoed voices certainly didn't help. At an instant, the lights came on, along with Agnes's voice. *There, I found the switch.*

We found ourselves in a circular room, surrounded by baroque furniture. The walls were black as the night. Eighteenth-century portraits were strewn about, mainly of women reposed in stately poses. Some were mad looking, as if they were suffering from sort of insanity. Based on the similarity of facial likeness, I assumed they were portraits of the previous owner's descendants. The house was constructed in the manner of a crucifix, with the main axis being the living room. This room was directly located beneath a low-projecting gable on the front. There were circular, polygonal bay windows throughout the house with ribbon art-glass casements. The windows had the effect of a stained-glass chapel. With the curtains drawn, the light would magnificently filter and fracture any incoming light, I thought. But, no, the owner would've had no use for sunlight. The interior of this gothic house spoke that truth very clearly. To achieve the two arms of the cross, the architect had placed a reception room and a dining room. To make this portion of the house even more striking, they had then elongated the arms of this cross by designing a carriage entry on one end and a screened porch on the other. In addition, the ceiling was situated at a height of sixteen feet, which was ideal for my height. It was a house unlike any other that I had seen. One felt transported to another era, where kings and queens reigned, where opulence was expected and appreciated. Agnes and I looked at one another and smiled. *"Grand, isn't it?"* she exclaimed. You could tell that even she had not expected this treasured listing. However, we both expected a shortcoming, something that would become manifest soon. The house was priced significantly less than market value in that part of Providence. We both recognized there must be a flaw in the structure of the house. I had conceded that even a death could not depreciate the value of the house to that extent. There had to be another reason for this. Agnes aimed to find out.

And that's when we glimpsed the handcuffs laid on the floor, about twelve feet from us. We looked at one another again, and, this time, we did not smile.

NADIA SULLIVAN,
ÉLAN VITAL:
A STUDY IN LIFE UNEXPAINED (EXCERPTS)

To make my theories "come to life," so to speak, I must apply my own life experiences to these theoretical concerns and premises. A brief history of my life, then, is in order.

I was born in Massachusetts Hospital in Boston, Massachusetts, as Nadia Sullivan. My biological father was Henry Sullivan, a prominent psychiatrist at that institution, who passed almost twenty years ago. My mother died during childbirth. There is no mention of her in my birth certificates or medical records. My father never discussed her identity or history with me, either. It is assumed that she was black (given my mixed skin color) and worked at the psychiatric ward where my father was a clinician and instructor of psychiatry. This is an assumption. I cannot locate any records of my mother at the hospital or elsewhere.

My father, Henry, who was of Irish descent, was quite prominent in the medical community in Boston. He was the Senior Attending in Psychiatry at Massachusetts Hospital for about a decade and had a robust following with the residents. Although my father relished all the cultural and intellectual delights that Boston had to offer, he appeared to have developed an acrimonious relationship with his mentor, Dr. Deutermann, a stout and bitter German psychiatrist (as people have told me), over the years. It's unclear how such a pleasant relationship, at least on the surface, turned so caustic that caused my father to resign as a physician at that hospital. Henry offered me no explanations about this matter. Subsequently, he accepted a position at The Miriam Hospital in Rhode Island to become the director of its psychiatry program there. I was nine years old when we left for Providence, a city that I still hold dear in my heart and in which I continue to reside. I remember my first smell of the marzipan bread wafting through the streets in the Fox Point neighborhood in Providence. I still go there frequently to relive that first experience, that bucolic setting. But I digress from the important matter at hand.

The Prohibition era, fueled by the passing of the Eighteen Amendment, as readers may be aware, illegalized the manufacture, transportation, and sale of alcohol. After my father left Boston, he felt depressed and undervalued at The Miriam Hospital, and, thus, began to become dependent on alcohol. Because he couldn't procure alcohol legally anymore, he would frequent the various speakeasies in Providence to drink his bourbon or whiskey. Although I was not yet a teenager, I could sense the desperation and loneliness he felt. He wasn't married and his vices were keen. I do not mean to besmirch his reputation, but he would solicit prostitutes and bring them home with him. At that point, he was so drunk that he could not fathom the hurt or disappointment that I may have felt. However, I weathered this bitter storm as best as I could and kept up with my studies more diligently than ever. I believe it was a defense mechanism of sorts, so that I could ignore what was really bothering me.

Whether voluntary or involuntary, my perseverance was ultimately rewarded with a scholarship to Yale University. Medical school at Harvard followed soon. Father was proud of me, although he eyed me suspiciously, as if I had special powers that I had not disclosed to him. I continued to have more diminished contact with him through the years, as I then entered my neurology residency with a post-doctoral work at Brigham & Women's Hospital. I never practiced clinical medicine, because I decided to enter the academic realm.

I returned home to Providence years later, as my father was growing older, and noticed that he had become a more belligerent alcoholic. He was much better at hiding his vices now than when I was younger, but his dependence on alcohol and sex would shine through at the most unexpected times. The frequency of his episodes of lashing out was less but more intense when they occurred. His demeanor and body told me so much. His face was consistently red now, from the enlarged blood vessels, the telangiectasia. His nose had also become swollen, red, and bumpy, a condition called rhinophyma. It would be a few years later at the apogee of his alcoholic addiction when he would begin to develop gastric ulcers and cirrhosis of the liver. Ultimately, my father would hemorrhage. He would die in my arms in our home in Providence. Even though he worked in hospitals for his entire career, he would refuse to depart this life in a hygienic, impersonal space. He belonged at home with his collection pornographic magazines and whiskey.

I knew so much about him, yet so little. He was

pathologically secretive. His past work at Massachusetts Hospital, before I was born, was closed off to me. The identity of my mother would be, too. Very few people attended his funeral, although he was well-known in Boston and Providence. I assume it was because of his alcoholism and the enmity that he had woven between himself and others throughout his last few years. People tend to forget the many years of good when they are confronted with the last several years of bad. My father was a great example of that.

By that time, I had converted to Islam, because the writings of the Quran had really resonated with me throughout medical school and residency. There was an innate calling within me to follow Allah's scriptures in the Quran. I had never been attracted to my father's stale Catholicism, which reeked of false idols and patriarchy. One could obviously say the same thing about Islam, but to me and if you read the Quran through a feminist perspective, you'll begin to understand that Islam gives women choices and respects them. In addition, I had a few Muslim friends whom I revered. They had guided my instincts and ethics throughout these years, and, so, I decided to follow their religious doctrine and way of life. From that point on, I donned a short hijab, a scarf, really, which did not seem so severe. Occasionally, individuals would look upon me as a foreigner, but people in Boston and Providence were sophisticated enough to understand.

On the day of Henry's funeral, I wore a longer hijab made of black lace. I shed a few tears for him but not what you would expect for a daughter. I had grown estranged from his European values and ideals. He did not instill in me any of the respect that I had shown him in my younger years. He was my old world. The new one would be just beginning. At the time of his death, my father no longer had any significant wealth. He had squandered most of it on alcohol and prostitution. However, I inherited our grand family home on 1111 Angell Street, in which I still reside. The home was superficially extravagant and opulent, with portraits of my father's maternal lineage hung around the house. One had the feeling they were talismans, so many in number, used for protection from the ghosts of our past. However, these only made me feel like the stranger I was. I felt so disconnected from my father's family. My mother's, I would never know.

However, in all its superficial grandeur, the home had flaws. The mahogany floors were not sturdy enough. Creaks could be felt throughout the home. Its walls were wafer-thin. Voices reverberated in the hollow spaces, as if ghosts from the past were speaking to us in distorted speeches from a future beyond. I surmised that many individuals had expired there. At night, I could hear whispers and echoes. But I could not distinguish whether these were coming from the chaos of my inner mind or the house itself.

Within that year, I accepted an academic position at Brown University and became the first faculty member in the Behavioral Neuroscience Department. It was the ideal position for me. It kept me busy and allowed me the freedom to carry out my research interests into memory and the origins and treatments for Alzheimer's disease, as my readers know. Life was uneventful. I was so immersed in my work that I kept to myself. I never married. I did not have relations with anyone. I know this may seem too much personal information to divulge, but I was still a virgin. My virginity would play a significant aspect in what I relate.

This was life until six months ago. The next chapter will be baffling for most. I hope you will not be detracted from my work as a behavioral neuroscientist for what I divulge. Yes, it may seem unbelievable. Undeniably, it will appear outlandish. But I trust that my readers will be able to understand that such marvelous, supernatural feats can indeed coexist with the mundane and scientific. I have nothing to gain from relating any of these things.

1996 | PROVIDENCE, RHODE ISLAND
THE MAN

Agnes and I approached the handcuffs like explorers in the forest advancing toward treasured artifacts that might be ensnared: cautiously but enthusiastically. It was so puzzling that these cuffs were laid there, as if they served as a clue to whatever mystery this house contained. Their placement in the living room just seemed so odd, too, as if staged for our entertainment. Both of us were perhaps thinking of a mine that would suddenly detonate and kill us. But the handcuffs were too alluring and too shiny to just observe from afar. We couldn't wait to examine them in more detail but were wary of any traps that would impede us along the way. We safely maneuvered our way toward them. She turned to me and said, *"Exquisite, isn't it? They look so byzantine and spectacular. It's just what I would expect in this house."* Agnes's vocabulary was always unexpected and brought a smile to my face. She, too, was a relic from the past, a sort of treasure in this college town that was all too stifling. I was fortunate to have found her.

"I agree," I said. *They look like they could be from the early 20th Century. Prison handcuffs, to be sure, but they're so ornately constructed. And they're gold. The individual who was restrained with them must have been some prisoner."* And that's when we also saw the accompanying cuffs for the legs. Agnes replied, *"Yes, some prisoner, indeed. I guess they had a difficult time containing them. These cuffs would hinder movement of any sorts."* We then laid these on the floor and began to observe the rest of the home.

The floors were composed of a very nice reddish mahogany wood. They looked in rather good condition. You'd be surprised to know that wood absorbs. Did you know that? It absorbs not only sounds but also events. Wood doesn't forget. One piece of the wood was worn out, as if it had been walked on too many times. There was a story there, but what? Expensive Persian rugs covered the wood. The exterior of the house belied what would be found within. The house's unkempt exterior appearance only made its interior appear expansive and regal. We walked to the spiral staircase, which was also constructed from mahogany. The staircase's trajectory was so circuitous, however, that we could not see where it led. For all we knew, it could be a dead end.

At that moment, I was reminded of the home of Sarah Winchester, the widow of firearm magnate William Wirt Winchester, who, after her husband's death, relocated to San Jose, California, and built a seven-story mansion. Legend has it that Sarah's remorse over the deaths caused by firearms made her continually build the home to appease these ghosts, to give them a residence in which to reside. The home also exhibited numerous oddities, such as doors and stairs that went nowhere, which were meant to confuse the ghosts from finding their way if they happened to be haunting Sarah.

Although most would've found Sarah's narrative depressive and delusional, I empathized with her and knew exactly what she would have felt. I absolutely believe in ghosts. My purchase of the current home, as I've stated, was contingent on the occurrence of a death therein. But, unlike Sarah, I cherished the idea of sitting with ghosts, reading with them, eating with them, playing card games with them. I wanted friends, and the dead seemed to be more forgiving than those who were alive. Contrary to popular belief, ghosts are just like any other humans and perhaps even better. They want to live their lives serenely in an after-life. They desire to be treated decently. Most prefer solitude—rest from the last seventy-plus years in which they were worked to the bone. Most of the ghosts that I had encountered were legitimately nice. They only became surly when humans offended them in some flagrant way. I have many stories to tell of ghosts. But we don't have time for that now.

Entering the home, I could not detect any unusual presence or spirits. This was not uncommon for me. I never had the natural ability to "sense" spirits when I entered a room. Those paranormal investigators who say otherwise are merely trying to appease their clients. No spirit entity presents itself to anyone without becoming familiar with its guests first. I never bought into the fact that Tangina Barrons, the spiritual medium in *Poltergeist*, could sense spirits as she walked into the Freeling's residence. As any legitimate investigator will tell you, that never happens. Spirits are shy, the shyest, perhaps. Even the showiest of them will ensure that those who seek it have a purpose and a spiritual aim. Spirits do not play games. Though they may have all the time for them, they regard them as purposeless. Contrary to what Tangina suggests in the film, spirits do not linger in a perpetual dream state. They are fully conscious. They are distinctly aware of whatever is occurring. They are intelligent and intuitive. Spirits perpetually engage in mindfulness. They are "present." Always. I've learned this from my many engagements with them.

At one point, Agnes had asked about my occupation. Once again, I had evaded any questions from her that would shed light into my personal life. She hadn't inquired more about it. She was instinctive that way, recognizing that I wanted to keep my life private. I don't know what she would have thought had I told her about my profession. She would probably find it "extraordinary," but I didn't want to provide anyone more information than I thought necessary. We approached the staircase, and ventured upstairs.

NADIA SULLIVAN,
ÉLAN VITAL:
A STUDY IN LIFE UNEXPLAINED (EXCERPTS)

Until six months ago, my life was quiet and unexceptional, as it had been for the past twenty years, when my father passed. I went about teaching my graduate courses in behavioral neuroscience and occasionally had small gatherings with the graduate students in the department. I was not particularly interested in my fellow colleagues in the department, nor did I associate with them. Most of them were affable but I kept to myself and my studies. I was determined to find a cure for Alzheimer's disease. I knew it wouldn't occur in my lifetime, but I was committed to making a significant headway. The little I could contribute would be worthwhile at the end.

As I said, everything was progressing as usual. In June of this year, I noticed that I was becoming fatigued with even the most routine activities. I also began to experience double vision and slight weakness in my arms, which occurred sporadically. I was fifty years old and healthy, with no significant medical problems or surgeries. I attributed this exhaustion to my research, as I would work excessive hours both at the lab and at my residence, often into the morning hours. I did not want to think about all the medical possibilities for my symptoms. Most physicians think they're invincible. They dismiss their symptoms, even those they should not ignore. I was certainly guilty of that. Because I did not have a husband or children and taught only two days of the week, I had absolute freedom. My irregular schedule worked for me. I was a night owl. I cherished the night and all that it brought, especially the creativity. My ideas soared. My aspirations took flight. However, my fatigue gradually worsened, and I could no longer dismiss my symptoms. Once I began to experience shortness of breath, I knew this was not just fatigue. It was something serious. I needed and sought out medical help.

I visited my internist at The Miriam Hospital, where my father had worked. A plain x-ray of my chest was taken that showed findings consistent with lung cancer. A subsequent biopsy of my lung revealed that it was non-small cell carcinoma, a lethal kind. At best, I had a five-year survival rate of about twenty-five percent. At worst, I would die within a few months. I don't know what I felt when I received the news. Part of me was relieved that there was an answer to what I was feeling. But part of me was immensely terrified of dying, this death that I had not ever seriously thought about. Sure, theoretically, I had contemplated it, but because I never took care of patients, I never brushed against it like other doctors had. At that moment, I knew that I would soon die and, at once, I felt pure exhilaration and profound despair. I would die alone, I thought. I knew there would be no one to hold my hand before I drew my last breath. My life would be tragic on the small screen. No one would disagree with that. But I also thought about all that was left open for me to explore. I could be disinhibited, like my father had been. I could be reckless. I could be another person, a Ms. Hyde to my Dr. Jekyll. What things

I could accomplish if I knew that I would die within a few months! How brazen my life would be! I would have no shame. I would have nothing to conceal. That is the route that I decided to follow, swiftly, without thought.

Briefly, I pondered my diagnosis. Although I wasn't a smoker, I can't say that I was significantly surprised by my diagnosis. I had not inquired into the insulation of our home until more recently, when I was informed that it was lined with asbestos. Ironically, the house on Angell Street, despite its name, would be my downfall, the cause of my death. I looked at the beautiful magnolias in the garden and thought of Plath's poem, *Paralytic*. I knew this was death. Like the claw of the magnolia, I did not ask—no, did not need—anything of life. I, too, like that sharp and dangerous lower part of the flower, was drunk on my own scents, attempting to start a hedonistic life on the verge of my demise. I would die in the same house as my father. We would be ghosts together. The thought of living with him sickened me, though I would be grateful that I had company.

While my doctor implored me to initiate chemotherapy, we both knew it was hopeless. It would perhaps offer me a month or so of living, but at what cost? Would I be living, anyway? I would lose my hair, vomit daily, and lose sensation in my feet. The choice was made. I would live freely until my last days. I would put on a performance for everyone. I would put on a brave face for all who cared to see me. I would be a different Nadia.

At the staircase of the "crucifix" house, as I've referred to it since I lay foot inside it, there were distinct paths for the three bedrooms. Two of the rooms were of similar size while the last was significantly larger. We looked at the two rooms that were alike. Both looked nondescript and featureless. They were about four hundred square feet each, with two windows. There was one closet in each room, but, based on the rest of the house, these rooms did not have any distinctive features. It was as if we were in a different home. Whereas the living and dining rooms were so opulent and grand, the two bedrooms had nothing special to convey. The walls were painted white, in contrast to the dining room and living space. There was no furniture within those spaces. They were bare and unassuming.

However, the last room was something else. It looked like an altar for Muhammad, the prophet of Islam. Although I had learned long ago that visual depictions of all prophets of Islam were usually prohibited, this room refuted this notion. A couple of the paintings had depicted the prophet with his face veiled. A solo one, which I found the most fascinating, had represented him with a burning flame, a flame that appeared to follow me everywhere. In most of the depictions, Muhammad had shoulder length hair, brown in color, with a green turban. In all the visuals, he was holding the Quran. He was not dissimilar to Christ in appearance. I wondered if this were the depiction for any prophet or Lord when their portrait could not be accurately known. Various Islamic prayer beads, called Tasbih, were also found on an ornate, wooden cabinet. Whoever had previously owned this home was, no doubt, a devout Muslim.

Walking into and through this home was like roaming through a funhouse mirror at Luna Park in Coney Island. The configuration was wild and strange. One didn't know what to expect in any of the rooms. Whether bare or replete with opulent items, one was never sure where they stood with this house. It was then that I felt a chill, a chill that I sense with the presence of spirits. Unlike what horror or ghost films depict, spirits cannot move objects, what we call telekinesis. The mind "moves" the object itself because that is what it desires to see.

With spirits, one feels a sensation of cold or heat, as if blood has been chilled or warmed. At times, the spirits meet in your gut, so to speak, and you feel an uneasy feeling, as if you're falling from a building. It can be exhilarating. It can be terrifying, but not in way you'd expect. Spirits often communicate in a manner with which we humans are not familiar. Sure, a Ouija board often works, but it's so elementary. If you're not trained in how to connect with the spiritual realm, you're opening a channel to all spirits. Messages become crossed. Energies get warped. Things fall apart.

The way I like to do it is to let the spirits be. You must be focused. You must reach out to an intended spirit. They'll answer you in a way they desire and that you understand. One should never be afraid of them. Sprits cannot harm you. You may get weird vibes from them, but they're benign. What I've learned over the years is that our spirits, at least part of them, still live here on earth when we die. And they are tethered more strongly to the earth when they are stuck here for some ulterior purpose, when they cannot move on.

Such was the spirit here. I could feel its energy, which was not malicious. It was friendly and forgiving. It wanted to guide me. It desired that l know something about it. This spirit had not completely moved the bulk of its energy to the other realm. It still had a purpose here. I could sense that very strongly.

NADIA SULLIVAN,
ÉLAN VITAL:
A STUDY IN LIFE UNEXPLAINED (EXCERPTS)

As you can imagine, with each day, I was worsening. I was becoming weaker. My double vision was becoming more troublesome. I was attempting to fight this illness alone. I was never one to ask for assistance from anyone because I was proud of my independence. I also didn't desire encroachment from anyone, especially during this illness. I wanted to be comfortable with my body, with my sickness, alone and unashamed. There were a few individuals in my neighborhood who knew about my diagnosis, but I attempted to remain as reclusive as I could. Vincent Duchene, a neighbor and surgeon at The Miriam Hospital, whose sitting-room window faced my bedroom's, was one such person who had inquired into my health. He had attempted to speak with me on various occasions. However, each time, I had said a quick hello and cordially dismissed him. I had briefly spoken to him about my cancer, but it was a curt and awkward discussion. He never ventured further.

One night, while undergoing a severe episode of double vision and feeling particularly drowsy, I had invited Vincent to my home, more out of politeness than anything else. I don't remember exactly what we spoke about, but it was probably a general conversation about the weather, about university life, or something trifle. I wasn't particularly in the mood and was so sleepy. I provided one-word answers to his questions, and he knew this was his cue to go. I excused myself to the bedroom and took several oxycodone tablets for my pain. I told Vincent to excuse himself. Before I knew it, the sun had risen, but all I could feel was a pain in my belly and vagina. I was dumbfounded with the litany and type of symptoms that this cancer brought. I also noticed blood on my sheets, which surprised me. However, I reasoned it was my hemoptysis, as I was coughing up more blood with each passing day.

My breathing was also becoming more labored now. Because of this, my internist had prescribed me an oxygen tank for the hypoxemia to use when I was physically active. I had reluctantly agreed with this intervention. Otherwise, I couldn't carry out any of my tasks, even those that were menial.

I passed my days reading Buddhist texts, the poetry of Omar Khayyam, and the Zabur. The Bhagavad Gita, especially, guided me during this time. I empathized with prince Arjuna and his moral dilemma regarding the violence and death that could ensue were he to engage in battle against his own kin. In that tale, the Hindu deity, Krishna, counsels the prince to uphold the war through selfless action. I wished I had my own counselor during this turbulent time. The ethical issues and philosophical themes that this scripture impressed upon me were at once too relevant and too restrictive. I wanted to fly away like a pure dove. I desired to leave my sinful body behind to do as it pleased. I decided to explore each of my facets, if you will, until I expired.

You would not be wrong if you considered me a prude. I was. But I wasn't ashamed of it. With this newfound freedom that my impending death brought, however, I felt a need to explore my darker nature. I would often disrobe in front of my bedroom window, so that my neighbor, Vincent, would keep a close surveillance on me. He appeared to be single, too, living in that large home. I believe his wife had passed away long ago. I pretended not to see him, but everything I did was for his him, for his gaze. At first, I removed my hijab, then slowly began to reveal my nightgown. I was a devout Muslim. In my Islamic faith, modesty and controlling one's desires are vital tenets. This was the most difficult thing for me to do. I believed that I had showed blasphemy to my faith. But this new sense of immodesty was absolutely exhilarating. I knew that someone was watching me undress. I would splay naked on my bed, with my legs spread apart, revealing my genitals in full display. If Allah could see me in this fashion, and he did, then how could I be saved? Another being, far more playful, far more dangerous than the cancer, had assumed my body and was taking liberties with it that I would not have dared. I had loved all that was pure and holy, but, now, I had yielded to something far more dangerous than those, this darkness that knew no limits. Confronted with the light and the dark, I chose darkness. Or, rather, darkness chose me.

It was on a particular night when I first experienced what would be one of several encounters with another entity, the only word that I know to describe it. I had just fallen asleep after a very fitful latency when I began to sense something extraordinary and unimaginable. I felt myself traveling through time and space, a galaxy of flashing stars. It was a very fluid motion, as if I were bypassing time while also recognizing the previous life that I may have lived. I cannot describe it better than that. I had no physical perception of anything. My senses had distilled into one. I could feel myself entering my mother's womb from an intermittent space, neither life nor death, but someplace more fluid and wavering, more even-tempered and comforting. I had a body now. I could sense a belly, fingers, feet. All my body parts had formed and coalesced perfectly. I then reached the birth canal, where I felt a darker presence, something that I had not felt while entering my mother's womb. I remained alert. I could see shadows of people circling my mother, who was screaming so forcefully. I heard her shout at me, "You're going to kill me, devil child. Leave me." I felt paralyzed, not knowing what to do. My mother clearly did not want me to be born, but I would die if I did not exit the womb. I realized this was the crucial decision I had to make. I could either live or die. Then, with a resolve and an extraordinary push that I have never felt before, I decided to exit her womb. I felt coldness around me, on my face, on my body. Then, a rush of cold air entered my lungs. I was born.

THE MAN

I told Agnes I had seen enough of the home. "I want to purchase it," I said. "It's exactly what I'm looking for. How soon can I sign the contract and move in? I'm willing to close escrow in two weeks. This will be an all-cash offer." Agnes was silent. She looked awkward this time, as if she didn't quite know how to respond. I hadn't seen her like this before. I let her remain so until she spoke. I didn't know what had altered her cheerful mood. Was it something I had said? She spoke: "I'm afraid the home can't be sold. I spoke with the agent while you were looking at the rooms…. the house can only be borrowed…from the ghost that has decided to remain here." I thought she was jesting about the borrowed part, but she was serious. "That is the contingent portion of the agreement. It is what the owner wanted," she continued. "You mean the owner who died in the home? "Yes, exactly," she said. "Isn't that what you wanted, that someone should have died in the home? Well, it appears that the deceased's estate also has a condition regarding the terms by which the home can be sold," she continued. "What if they didn't die and will return to claim the home? Perhaps this is a trick," I replied, knowing that I was being paranoid. "Rest assured that no one is returning to this house," she jovially said, "of that I can be certain. Of course, the price of the home will remain the same, and you'll still have access to it. So, essentially, you'll still be the owner in the physical realm, but not the spiritual realm."

I smiled at that part. "And that is the reason the house is being sold at a significantly lower price," she resumed. She smiled lightheartedly. Agnes could be serious when she wanted to be. But, for the most part, she had a playful and refreshing nature.

Agnes carried one of those new Motorola clamshell phones, which stood out against her rather modest appearance. It was very jarring. The new and the old, the soft body against the hard gadget. "Well," I started, "can we find out the owner's name? I think that request about borrowing the house is very strange, don't you, Ms. Winterbottom?" "Yes, absolutely," she replied. "I have the owner's name here. She was a professor of behavioral neuroscience at Brown. Her name is Nadia Sullivan. As I said before, she died in this house in 1970 and it has been unoccupied since that time. I guess, for most people, a death in the home is not very enticing when it comes to its purchase. It's a deal breaker. Unfortunately, I have no more information about her or how she died or, if we believe the myths, where her body disappeared. You may have some success at Brown. I'm sure the faculty there can shed some light on the matter." She looked at me with her soft glare and smiled again. It wasn't a mocking smile but a cordial one. I understood her, and she understood me. "We'll have the papers drawn up very quickly. Because we're not negotiating the price or asking for an inspection or any improvements, and the offer is all cash, there shouldn't be any issues with the sale of the home," she said. "Thank you for your help, Ms. Winterbottom," I replied. "Please call me

Agnes. It was very nice to meet you. This was my quickest sale yet. Thank you for the opportunity," she replied. "The pleasure is all mine," I responded. And that was the truth.

Each day, the cancer was taking its toll on my body. Each day, my body was being more fully invaded by this other higher power. Vincent was even more engrossed in my drama. I could see him reclining in his chaise lounge chair, and, with his eyes, he was undressing me and making love to me. It was pleasurable, to say the least, that someone would desire me, especially in my wretched state. I felt his hands caress my bosoms gently while biting my nipples. I felt his wet lips on my parched ones, while he panted slowly. He then guided his hands onto my genitals, pleasurably massaging them. I could sense all of this, as if it were physical. I kept telling myself: Never let them in. Don't let these evil thoughts enter your pure soul, Allah's sacrosanct domain. But I was too powerless against this lust that had blossomed, it seems, slowly over the years.

I felt that an evil spirit had infused itself within me, provoking me with carnal lusts. I had to stifle that desire, starve that fever. Was it the jinn I had read so much about? Allah would not be pleased. Based on what one of the Imams had told my friend with a similar problem in the past, I must do two things to rid myself of the jinn. I must plunge verses of the Quran into a bowl of clean water, and then pour the holy water over my head. That would instantly drive away the spirts, that Imam had said. To continue to keep the spirits at bay, I would have to say my prayers five times a day and wear my hijab. I vowed that I would do this. Occasionally, I would see shadows of a man outside my home, lurking closer and closer each time. Was this the jinn that I feared or was this my double vision playing tricks on me? To quiet my mind and to capture their souls in photography, I decided to take photos of these shadows when I saw them.

One night, I felt particularly strange, as if my body had been removed from itself. I was like a rattle snake, rubbing my skin against a rough surface to shed it. I was molting. Everything was in a haze, as if I were not there. I felt drugged, under ether. However, through my laced curtains, I felt Vincent's gaze upon me even more intensely. It was early morning and I had just fallen asleep. Oh, how I relished this: being loved, something that my father had never bestowed upon me. Then it happened: I felt Vincent on the ceiling above me, as a shadow, although he was also observing me through the windows. Unlike previous times, I didn't have a physical sensation that he was on top of my body or that he had penetrated me. There was no foreplay. There was no lovemaking. I could see him hovering above me, touching the high ceilings, while also sensing his gaze across from my windows. It seemed like he had two forms, a physical one and a shadowy doppelgänger. I felt expanded, as if my stomach was increasing in size. This expansion was both physical and emotional. I was now outside my body looking in. I, too, had a darker shadow that had merged with that of Vincent's. We were both one now. An uncomfortable electrical current traveled down my spinal cord. It galvanized me. Next, a very soft light flashed through me, and inflated me further without the weight of the previous expansion. My intuition was that I had just conceived, although I knew this was impossible. Vincent and I had never had a physical encounter, let alone any meaningful conversations with one another. Yet, there was an emotional encounter between us, a security that I felt when Vincent gazed upon me.

I awoke the following day, feeling nauseous. I detected that I had dreamt the entire episode, but I also realized that something was different within me. Something or someone else was residing within me now. I perceived a presence. Realizing that I may have conceived, however improbable that was, I decided to undergo a serology test four weeks later. The test was affirmative for a pregnancy. The internist was incredulous on two accounts. First, she could not fathom as to my reasons for desiring to conceive under such circumstances, when I was diagnosed with such a malignant form of cancer. I would certainly die before I birthed the infant. That, she told me. Second, she could not explain how I could conceive given my age. I was fifty years of age, and although not impossible, the gestation was unlikely and, more significantly, dangerous. She looked at me, at my recklessness and irresponsibility. My physician was resolved that this child would be aborted by my body. It would not be viable, she gathered. She could not fathom that my body would allow this child to be born. She didn't ask about the child's father or any of the usual questions that one would ask under these unusual circumstances.

She realized that I was extremely private about my personal affairs. I thanked her and left her office, fully cognizant that I was pregnant, yet realizing this could not be possible. I sensed a tug, as if the universe were pulling and pushing me, back and forth, to determine my strength through this miraculous ordeal.

1996 | PROVIDENCE, RHODE ISLAND
THE MAN

I borrowed the keys to the crucifix house from Agnes. I primarily wanted to go there and gather more information about the occupied spirit that I had sensed there several days ago. I went there just before midnight. Over the years, I've deduced that spirits are more favorable and receptive at night. There are two reasons for this. First, spirits have no circadian rhythm. This is unlike us humans who are alerted by daylight, our zeitgeber, the cue that entrains or synchronizes are biological rhythms to the Earth's cycle. Second, we, ourselves, are more receptive to spirits in the nocturnal hours. During night, we're in a more relaxed state and can "take in," if you will, various wavelengths of energy. You may think that I'm ridiculous, but these facts are also based in science. I can assure you of that.

I ventured to the house on a wet and windy summer night. The house looked different at night, but not what you would expect from horror films. It looked like it needed help, as if someone were abusing it. Its windows looked like eyes, large and inquisitive. Its frame looked like a body, solid but withering ever so slowly. The shabby and clawed door was its mouth, being silenced before it had a chance to speak. It called to me, but I couldn't exactly decipher its message. Perhaps the spirit was anxious to speak to me. I hurried up the staircase.

All the elements were poised to give me the best chance of the encounter with the spirit. If someone had seen me enter that semi-grisly house that night looking the way I do, they would have thought I was the monstrous inhabitant of that abode. Under these circumstances, the house suited my grotesque appearance to a T. I'd also brought a bottle of Bowmore's single malt scotch whiskey, my go-to liquor, especially in times of loneliness and desolation. Some matches, candles, paper, and pen were also in-hand. I had planned to engage in automatic writing or psychography.

If you're not familiar with this practice, I recommend it, especially if you're trying to communicate with your dead relatives. Better than a Ouija board, automatic writing places the spirit in your writing hand so it can direct what it's communicating. You can't learn this process overnight. Rather, you must allow some dissociation from yourself, so the spirit can guide your hand. But, first, some unwritten rules that I've learned over the years. First, don't test a spirit. This is not an exam or a pop quiz. They'll be annoyed as hell. They will purposely provide you with wrong answers and fail, you, rather dramatically and comically. Second, don't ask questions to which you already know the answers. Testing a spirit this way demeans the process and is an exercise in futility. Third, don't ask "yes" or "no" questions. On the other extreme, your questions cannot be open-ended or lengthy. They should be directed and specific. Your answer, in turn, will be curt and precise. But it may also be vague. Be prepared. Fourth, realize that you can't get a spirit to make decisions for you, either. They are not your guide or oracle. And, last, have an open mind. Start a session knowing that your expectations may be uprooted and reformed. There are no limitations or bounds in the spirit world.

Like you, I was skeptical, especially in the beginning sessions. I had trained with a spiritualist in the last city I lived, Hollywood, California, and was immediately turned off by it. To me, the process was a sham, and I thought my spiritualist was a mountebank. I was in Tinsel town, too, which made the entire thing suspicious. Being amid the backdrop of a Hollywood sign or the Universal Studios lot didn't bolster the legitimacy of the situation. But I stuck with it and it began to work. I was reawakened, as they say. The process was legitimate. I began to think about all my dead relatives with whom I wanted to converse, which, frankly, wasn't many. My grandfather, Lucas, came to mind and that was the first person I contacted. Most of the information that I gathered from his soul was truthful, but the rest I couldn't verify. However, my hand guided me; I didn't guide it. My skepticism quickly waned. Over the years, I have used psychography to connect with other souls. I became quite an expert of it in Los Angeles. It was side job, though, as I didn't want this to detract from my profession as a chemist.

It was with this arsenal of learned knowledge, whiskey, candles, paper, and writing utensils that I approached the home on 1111 Angell Street. I knew the questions that I would ask. I knew what I wanted from this soul that had traveled the underworld. If this were the soul with whom I would spend eternity, I would have to be gracious and kind, yet probative. I had already gathered that Nadia Sullivan's presumed soul was inviting and benevolent, but I had so many more questions to ask of it. It was like being on a first date with an individual with whom you'd be spending an eternity.

I opened the door of the house, which now seemed less formidable than the first time I was there. I switched on the lights and went up the stairs to the third room, where an homage was made to Muhammed. I then turned off those lights, lit the candle, and began the session, willing to let the spirit guide my left hand.

1996 | PROVIDENCE, RHODE ISLAND
THE MAN
PSYCHOGRAPHY SESSION WITH NADIA SULLIVAN

(Candle is lit; wind whistles; rain patters)

THE MAN: I'm attempting to summon Nadia Sullivan's spirit. Before I begin, I want to make sure that I'm channeling *her* spirit. I request a response. Apologies in advance if I'm trying to pin you down, as we say.

SPIRIT: This is Nadia's spirit. You must be prepared for these responses. The sprit roams. It cannot be pinned down, as you say. Your response is amusing though stale. I reside here in this former abode. You have borrowed the home from me, I hear.

THE MAN: Yes, you've heard correctly. I wish to be a spirit in this home. However, I do not mean to occupy your space. I merely want to know what keeps you here. What prevents most of your spirit from departing this earth?

SPIRIT: You speak of many sprits. I have one spirit. It is here. It is now. I cannot depart. I have a message to convey to a loved one in a physical form. My story is in my last written work where books are kept. Heed to that message. It will tell you all you need to know.

THE MAN: You, kind sprit, must also know the reason why I'm also here. I'm not asking whether I should kill myself or not. I plan on it. But I must inquire about my intent to kill myself. I hold myself accountable for my late wife's death.

SPIRIT: You ask what you should not. Regardless, the answer to your life can also be found in that book. You don't always need eyes to see.

(Candle is extinguished)

My automatic writing session with Nadia's spirit was not as illuminating as I hoped it'd be, but, nevertheless, it provided me with some clues of where to find more answers. Surely, her reference to where books are kept was a library. I would start there.

The confession I made regarding the death of my wife, undoubtedly, surprised and rattled you. May she rest in peace. This is the regrettable part that I left out. Forgive me. I'm not especially proud about that aspect of my life. Her death is the reason I left frenetic Hollywood for the tranquility of Providence. I needed to leave that desolate part of my life behind and bury it. I secretly buried my wife and our dead fetus before I departed. Hers was an unfortunate death. Our fetus's, a coffin birth.

But let's go back a decade ago to our beautiful history together that would soon turn tragic. I met my wife, Catherine, one sultry, sunny afternoon at Universal Studios. I had just arrived in California from Iowa and wanted to experience the glimmer and fantasy of Hollywood. A studio tour, where Hitchcock's *Psycho* and Spielberg's *Jaws* were filmed, seemed like the ideal place to start. Catherine worked there as a character actress, dressed up as the Bride of Frankenstein. She was a far better version of Elsa Lanchester's titular character. When I first saw Catherine, she was greeting and meeting guests at the park, with her long, simple white gown and cape. Her black-wedged, cotton candy-like hair, with the sinusoidal streak of white, was celestial. She wore a blood-dark lipstick and looked like she had killed someone and sucked their blood. She was my version of perfected beauty, a femme fatale. Although I was looking at her sideways, hoping that she would not see me, Catherine was too smart for that. She excused herself from her guests and came towards me, saying: "So, I'm no longer good enough for you, my Frankenstein?" She then laughed nonchalantly, as was her usual way, and offered me her hand to kiss. "Enchanté," she exclaimed. "My name is Catherine, your Bride." I kissed her hand, reflexively, not knowing how to continue. Was I being mocked in a sort of Universal Studios show that I didn't know about? The park usually had these types of impromptu entertainment. I certainly looked as grotesque and monstrous as a Frankenstein, and so this banter could make for a good show. A ridicule. However, Catherine whisked me away to the corner of an alley in a simulated version of Florence, Italy, held my face securely, and kissed me on the lips for ten seconds. She was actually fairly tall, standing at 5'11 inches, but I still had to crouch a great deal to reach her lips. Was this all a hallucination of a Hollywood fantasy? A hideous creature kissing a beautiful, exotic bride? At that moment, I couldn't decide, but I knew that I didn't want it to end. I was truly in La La Land.

Flash forward to a year ago, when I landed a respectable position as a chemist at Caltech in Pasadena, researching molecular configurations of amphetamine and methamphetamine. I was attempting to decipher the role that the addition of CH3 would have on the former. What led to its changes of thought processes and mood? Because my salary had increased, Catherine no longer had to work. She was happily resigned to be a wife and a future mother.

Those years with Catherine were the best days of my life. Truly. I, who looked like a beast, had found a beautiful wife and a rewarding career. I awoke to the sun every day. I returned home in balmy weather, passing palm trees and joggers decked out in their Adidas workout clothes and listening to their Sony Walkmans. I slept every night with the woman I loved. It could not be more blissful. Catherine and I loved each other immensely and soon realized that we had excess love to bestow upon a child. We contemplated this decision very carefully, fearing that our child could potentially inherit the gene for Marfan's. I recognized that there was a fifty percent chance of such an occurrence. Despite this, Catherine was content that this child would be loved regardless of their outward appearance. I was leery of this, knowing the stigma of the condition, but in the end, I begrudgingly acquiesced. Undoubtedly, we would love our child no matter what.

Initially, Catherine had difficulty conceiving due to her age (she was 48 years old), but we timed her menstrual cycle just right and adhered to strict rules regarding intercourse. It worked. We anticipated little Emma's birth nine months later.

The next nine months were joyful but by no means easy. From the onset, Catherine's pregnancy was riddled with severe nausea, vomiting, weight loss, and dehydration, what doctor's call hyperemesis gravidarum. During her first trimester, she was taken to Huntington Hospital in Pasadena, several times for intravenous hydration. I could tell that despite her love for this fetus, she wanted to give up and die. She told me that several times. But I knew those were her moments of weakness, that her strength outweighed these minor obstacles. She hung on. Her second trimester was, for the most part, unremarkable. Then the problems started again, three months later. She began to experience swelling of her extremities. She complained of headaches. She would occasionally see double. I attributed all of these to her pregnancy, without realizing that something else could be the culprit. A month before her anticipated delivery, Catherine had one seizure, which obviously devastated us. Thankfully, it was limited in duration. She was given a diagnosis of eclampsia and her doctor ascribed this to her elevated blood pressure.

As the delivery date loomed, I realized that Catherine's physicians were not doing their job adequately. She was always sick. She was always on the verge of a breakdown. I was not a supporter of the medical establishment and became more distrustful of it during Catherine's pregnancy. Moreover, I did not want my baby girl to be born in an institution where she could be stolen or swapped for another child. Yes, I'd watched a lot of films about kidnappings and switched babies at birth in the hospital, but from the outset, I was against the birth of our child there. We compromised and decided to have the delivery at home with the use of a midwife. My departed mother was a midwife in Sussex,

England, (where I lived until I was eighteen years old), and she always told me that births at home brought the family together in ways that one could not imagine. Midwifery was linked to a decreased cesarean rate, a lower rate of induction, and decreased risk of preterm birth. My arguments worked. Catherine assented to it.

On the day that Catherine's labor began, she and I appeared calm and collected, but, inside, we were both a mess. No one wanted to confess to it, though. During those moments, I realized I may not have made the best choice in wanting to have the birth at home. The midwife, Lavinia, an older woman from Romania, seemed adept but a little too distant. She didn't have any emotional rapport with my wife, as one would expect. When Catherine's contractions became more regular and spaced closer together, we called Lavinia, to no avail. She was nowhere to be found. Her phone had been disconnected, and we didn't know where she lived. I think I had my first panic attack then but tried to conceal it for poor Catherine. She was calmer than I was, but I could see that she resented me at that moment. "Promise me," she said in a rather subdued tone, "that if things go south, you'll take me to the hospital." I wanted to calm her down, so I lied a little. "I'm more adept than you think, dear," I responded. "I've delivered many babies while living with my mother."

In truth, I had no experience in childbirth, but I had seen my mother deliver babies in our living room for most of my childhood. It didn't seem so complicated, I reasoned. I had learned several methodical steps from her that were instilled in my brain for eternity. First, wash your hands. My mother had been meticulous about hygiene. That was her thing. Wash, disinfect, wash some more, disinfect more. It served her well throughout the years. Second, be calm. Birth is natural, and the body knows how to do this. It's programmed within it. And, last, grab a bucket of warm water and clean towels to wipe the baby down and keep her warm. Position is also important, such as being propped up with pillows. I gathered all the necessary items and was ready for the delivery of our infant.

The baby was crowning. Catherine was in so much pain, but I tried to remain calm and confident. "We'll get through this," I kept saying. "It'll be all right." But she kept yelling, "Fuck, fuck, fuck, why did I agree to this? I knew this was a..." Suddenly, midway through her sentence, she stopped talking. She lost consciousness and began to seize, while she started to bleed voluminously through her uterus. I didn't know how to proceed. This continued for several minutes until her seizure stopped. Feeling relieved, I took her pulse. She didn't have any. Her breathing was also slowing. I just stood there, mentally and physically shut down. I couldn't do anything. And, even if I could, I didn't, as if I knew any interventions would be futile at that moment. But I knew that I had forgotten something. I had been negligent. And the hemorrhaging continued. I remained frozen. Eventually, after several more minutes, Catherine stopped breathing, her heart ceased to function, and she died. At that point, I didn't know if our infant, Emma, would survive. I waited a few minutes, until Catherine's body suddenly extruded the fetus. Emma, too, was dead, a languid ball of dead tissue. She looked like a fetus, the ones you see in textbooks, not quite formed and not quite human. She looked unreal. I didn't know what to do after having lost my beautiful wife and infant. I mean, place yourself in my position. What would you do? Well, the next few minutes decided my course of action, which I regret to this day.

My thoughts had slowed but my actions were fast. It was as if my body and mind had been somehow severed and the synapses were no longer communicating. I didn't know how to proceed. We had no family in the area. I had no real friends that I could contact, either. I was alone again, such as I had been before I had met Catherine. My heart sunk. This is what utter desolation feels like, I thought. When you have everything and lose it all, what remains? How do you go on? How do you survive this blow? It's too difficult to start over again. No, I didn't have that stamina in me anymore. Catherine was special. I couldn't hope to find another individual like her whom I could love so unconditionally. At that point, I knew my life was over.

What would I do with the bodies? Should I call the police, I thought. Wouldn't it look suspicious that I had tried to help with the birth of my own child? Hadn't I stopped all medical interventions and been negligent in my wife's care? Why hadn't I called 911, as I had promised Catherine? Why had I been so careless? Any fool would've tried to call the ambulance. And I, a researcher at Caltech, could not have been such an idiot and overlooked this, could I? I would be interrogated with all these questions. My responses would be subpar and not intelligible. Even I could foresee this. What could I really say to the police that would make me not look guilty and criminally negligent? Fear had already instilled itself so tightly in me that I was suffocating and couldn't think logically at all.

I quickly decided that I would bury them both but then changed my mind. I had no tools. I could not shovel dirt, for the life of me. And I didn't know where to bury them. It was as if my mind was thinking of all the scenarios, but it wasn't as fast as my hands or feet that decided my choices for me. It was the battle between fight or flight, and my body had chosen the latter. I then decided to cut their bodies and dispense them. How did I think of this idiotic plan? I don't know. Maybe it was because of all the horror films I had watched. Like I mentioned, my arms and hands were doing the thinking. My brain remained stagnant, frozen in time.

Catherine and I lived on the fourth floor of an apartment building, without an elevator. How could I hope to carry her body, which was literally dead weight, down those flight of stairs without arousing suspicion? I couldn't. Automatically, my hands did what my mind wouldn't even contemplate. I dragged Catherine's body on the old mahogany floor. There was so much blood, as much as in a Universal Studios horror flick. The smell was overpowering, redolent of iron and rust, reminiscent of the time I had toured a horse stable as a child when the mare had just given birth. How I wished this was a dark film in which I was an actor instead!

I dragged her corpse to the bathroom, which had a tub in it. Catherine's body weighed more than I expected. But because of an adrenaline surge, I was bionic and insurmountable. Physically, I could do anything but, mentally, I was severely challenged. With determined energy, I lifted her body and placed it there. I knew that I must burn this body, burn it out of my mind, and be done with it, once and for all. Catherine and I had several bottles of sulfuric acid in the bathroom that we used to clean our drain. This will do, I thought. I poured and kept pouring the acid on her face and body. Her body parts were being defaced beyond recognition. The first part was done. I liked that I could no longer identify the face or body as Catherine's. The anonymity of the body would make the rest of the sequences easier. However, the most gruesome tasks lay in store for me. I had watched too many films, so I took my cue from those. Later, I would sever her body parts into tiny pieces, bundle them, and place them in Hefty trash bags. Emma's body would be next to Catherine's. I would take these to Lake Hollywood, rent a boat, and dispense them there. I say all these things nonchalantly, but it had to be that way. The grisly details have been omitted from this story. Catherine and Emma deserved a proper burial, but given the circumstances, this was the best I could do. They would be buried in Hollywood, like the stars they were. Fortunately, or unfortunately, Catherine was a loner and an orphan like I was, so she would have no one, expect for me, to mourn for her. From a logistical aspect, that would make things so much simpler for me. But it was all so heartbreakingly unbearable, beyond anything I could have imagined!

The following day, I asked for a leave of absence from Caltech, lying to my boss that my mother had passed. I had to go to the East Coast to arrange for her funeral and handle her messy affairs, I told her. My boss gave me her warmest regards and wished me a speedy return. Little did

she know that my disappearance would be for good, that I
was planning to kill myself, that I really was as monstrous
as I looked.

Escrow on the home on Angell Street had not yet closed, so I spent a week at a B & B here in Providence, called Christopher Dodge House. It was pleasant enough. The calm of the inn, however, contrasted with the unrest in my mind. I had developed illusions and hallucinations, something that had not yet occurred after one of my psychography sessions. At breakfast, I would often see what I imagined were Nadia's large eyes in the yolk of the egg. The yellowness reminded me of her presumed halo. The gunky sediment of the French press signaled her dark past from which she could not extricate herself. In short, the session with Nadia's spirit had wrecked me both physically and emotionally and had brought me back to my demons. I could not think straight, and, when I thought, it was about Catherine, Emma, or Nadia. I could not sleep. Did I truly want to know if I was the cause of my wife's death? Was I ready to accept the fact that I had killed her, however unintentionally? What if her death were bound to happen, regardless of my inactions? The thought of knowing that I was at least some way responsible for her death prevented me from contacting Catherine's spirit. It was so much easier to know that, in theory, I had nothing to do with her death. The thought gnawed at me constantly.

I finally decided that the thought of not knowing the truth would eventually destroy me. I had to act on it because the answer could have some relevance for my future. In whatever manner this played itself out, I was destined to die, one way or another. Isn't that the reason I had left Los Angeles for the charmingly quaint city here, to kill myself? Nadia's spirit had indirectly stated that the answers I sought would be found in books, likely hers. She did not mention whether that was a published work or not. But I surmised that it was published or, at least be able to be located. With this, I decided to try The John Hay Library at Brown University where her books could be located.

The contents of the library had recently been archived in the world wide web. Although I was a chemist, I was never adept at technology. Call me a Luddite, but a part of me liked to grasp things and know they existed. The other part, as you know, shunned anything tangible or organic. The world wide web was caught in sort of a middle ground: I didn't like the composite of hardware and software. Give me one or another, but not both. I reviewed Nadia's works and saw that, throughout her career, she had only written two texts, both of which were seminal and consistently used as course readings at Brown and other universities. Her first book, *The Decay of Consciousness,* was considered groundbreaking for its time. It was written in the 1960s and discussed the antithesis of the Descartian "cogito, ergo sum." It proposed that the mind can outthink itself and create a new reality that is not predicated on knowledge or thought. That's what the summary said. The second book was neurologically based and discussed the various pathologies related to the temporal lobe of the brain. The pathologies that this book discussed were wild: Capgras syndrome, a cognitive-dysmnesic phenomenon in which individuals have an irrational belief that someone they know or recognize has been replaced by an imposter; Klüver-Bucy, a behavioral impairment characterized by inappropriate sexual behaviors and mouthing of objects. The list of these fascinating disorders went on. The name of this second book was certainly more playful. It was titled, *Looking for Imposters: The Limits of the Temporal Lobe*. Her biography mentioned that she was at work on her third book about Alzheimer's Disease, which was not published. There had to be more. None of those two books appeared to be the one that would provide me with answers to her riddle.

Armed with this bit of knowledge about Nadia, I ventured out to the library. The atmosphere of the university was suffocating, to say the least. I realized that I did not miss my university school days in Iowa. Although most Brown students dressed in regular clothes, a few groups stood out conspicuously: those with the Brown sweatshirts and t-shirts were obnoxiously annoying, as if they wanted to announce their resume on their chests and sleeves. It was nauseating. Then there were the rebels, the goths, who declared they were anti-establishment and against anything remotely academic. However, in their black attire they meant to suggest, "I'm not studious, but I'm intelligent, nonetheless." In their cool demeanor, they hinted at the fact that they would not be at Brown if not for their parents' cajoling. A third group was the prepsters, those who relished everything Ivy. They knew they were meant to be Ivy-educated from the moment they could think, but they did not want to be pigeon-holed into any one of the Ivies. They were all eight universities combined: A bit of Yale here, a bit of Princeton there, and so forth, but yet managed to still distill a Brown distinctiveness. I'm sure these types of groups can be found in any university, but at Brown, it was even more polarized and glaring.

The edifice of The Hay was beautiful. It was both classic and modern, with elongated columns comprising the exterior. When entering it, one felt that one was in an institution of higher learning. It somehow made one smarter. The library had a special collections rooms, where archives, rare books, and manuscripts were housed. However, as I had previously read, The Hay was one of the three Sacred Libraries on campus, which meant that nothing could be checked out of the building. Given this stipulation, I knew that Nadia's last, unpublished manuscript was here. It was just a guess, given the circumstances. I decided to test my theory.

THE MAN

I walked over to the reference desk where a grey-haired librarian was sitting. I would venture that she was at least 80 years old, although she looked bright-eyed and sharp. She was the epitome of a typical librarian: Bespectacled, slightly short, very bookish, and taciturn. A mystery shrouded her, as I began to wonder what kind of life she had lived. She asked for my ID card. I showed her my photograph identification card from Caltech, with my name crossed out, and told her that I was conducting research for my next scientific article. Most universities had some reciprocity between each other. She admitted me to the inner sanctum of the library, briefly looking at my card. I questioned her about Nadia Sullivan's manuscript. I didn't even know if one existed, but I had to ask. If not here, then where? What were my other choices? The librarian's name was announced with a desk name plate: Ms. Millie Hudson, Brown University Librarian. "Excuse me, Ms. Hudson," I said, "I'm looking for Professor Nadia Sullivan's manuscript, the last one she wrote before her death. I was told it was here." She glanced up at me from her pince-nez, first shocked at my monstrous appearance, I'm sure, and then annoyed that I was asking her a question. I saw the book she was reading: a Patricia Highsmith novel called *The Price of Salt*. I hadn't read it, but, given her annoyance, it must have been a damn good book. It took her a few seconds, but she got her bearings and looked at her computer screen. I hadn't been to a library since they started using computers with web connections. I had graduated from university adept at microfiche readers, but the world wide web was another organism altogether. "Let me see if we can find something, Mr...?" she said. As you know by now, I didn't give my name away nor did I respond to her question for fear of being identified or followed. She must have assumed that I was a professor of some sort, but she didn't inquire further. That was a good sign. "Well, the computer says there is a manuscript that was offered to us in 1971. The circumstances of it are a bit unclear, though. It was presented to the special collections by another individual," she said. My remark to her ambiguous response: "Would you have the manuscript here in the library?" She replied, "Well, it says it should be here. Let me look." At this point, her "wells" were annoying the hell out of me. It felt like I was hunting for treasure, a special object that I must find simply because it could not be discovered. She returned after looking at the collection. "It appears the manuscript is missing for some reason. However, the good news is that it must be here somewhere. As you know, nothing in this library can be checked out. It must remain in circulation here. Perhaps, it has been misplaced. I would just look for it if I were you." I was annoyed at this point. I replied, very begrudgingly: "Do you mean that her manuscript can be *anywhere*? Where do I even start?" She noted my annoyance and remarked: "The Hay is relatively small, and the manuscripts are bound very differently than the other books. It shouldn't take that long to find. I wish I could be more help, but that's the best I can do. I'll look out for it, too." I wanted to wring her neck at that moment but took a deep breath instead. I knew that I needed a class on meditation. "Cheers," I said, although I didn't mean it, and continued to look for that elusive manuscript.

THE MAN

I spent the next two weeks at The Hay looking for Nadia's manuscript or anything connected to it. It was agonizing. Every day, I felt a little closer to finding it, only to realize it was a false hope. I was convinced this manuscript was a chimera: that although it existed in theory, it could never be located. It felt like hunting for the original Holy Grail, the cup purportedly used by Jesus at his Last Supper. I wanted this manuscript so badly. What would it say, I wondered? Why had Nadia's spirit attached so much importance to it? Would it change my destiny? I suppose I could have had another psychography session with Nadia to ask the whereabouts of her text, but if she had wanted me to know, she would've told me. She wanted me to hunt for it. I had learned that spirits tell you what they want to tell you, no more, no less. In fact, you can upset them and easily sever a perfect relationship if you're too solicitous or questioning. As far as spirits are concerned, the squeaky wheel never gets the grease. Ever.

Toward the end of my two weeks at The Hay, I met a fellow by the name of Thurston, a graduate student at Brown specializing in the humanities of some sort. I forget. His name was from such a bygone era that I assumed he was from an aristocratic family. After all, who would name their child Thurston? That name didn't seem becoming of anyone. I know he had his eye on me, but I didn't know what he wanted. He was awfully curious but, after having butchered Catherine's corpse (good God, did I really do that?), I had feared that a team of FBI agents had been surveying me. It's crazy, I know. But I also realize that it's a completely normal reaction in such an abnormal situation.

In perusing any manuscripts that could shed a light on Nadia's monograph, I had come across an article by a Sarah Michelson that referenced Nadia's work. Michelson's article analyzed an aspect of Stevenson's *The Strange Case of Dr. Jekyll and Mr. Hyde* with a small footnote mentioning Nadia's work. This was a propitious sign, as I knew that Nadia's manuscript was tangible and real.

Thurston was very helpful, but he was just so insistent in getting to know me and what I wanted from this library. He appeared to be a smart, inquisitive kid. I think he was trying to figure me out: my background, my story, my interest in the manuscript. But I was resolved in showing him nothing. At first, he seemed obsequious but that was just his nature. He couldn't help it. I could tell that he was a loner but that, underneath it all, he desired company and someone to talk to. Although he was affable, he also gave me the impression of being somewhat depressed. I knew the signs too well. After Catherine's death, I was taking Prozac myself, which gave me the energy to do things that I couldn't have done, like searching for an elusive manuscript. Thurston showed those signs but hid them well. The fact that he tried to know me, appearing the way I do, made me warm up to him. I even allowed him to look for the manuscript with me, all the while not letting him know about its importance. After all, what would I say? That during the automatic writing session with a previous professor's spirit, I was told that her manuscript could have implications for my life and the crime that I had committed?

I was at my wit's end. I truly was. The manuscript was nowhere to be found. Even with Thurston's help, I wasn't any closer. Besides looking at any and every section of the special manuscripts, I had also begun to examine every other section in the library. If I'd been a burglar there, alone, the bookshelves would've all been hurled down, the books in disarray, examined in every crevice, until I found that elusive text. But here I was, in one of the most pristine libraries, while a couple of students were reading attentively with a librarian in the midst. What could I do? I wanted to scream and punch things. I wanted to kill myself for having done nothing for Catherine when she was dying, for not saving baby Emma. And then for cutting up both of their bodies. Oh, how I desired to die at that moment! The manuscript edged me on, however. Was there something in there, as Nadia's spirit had insinuated, which would help me?

Millie, the librarian, had kept a close eye on me during the past two weeks. She was the sole person behind the desk, from when The Hay would open to when it would close. I saw no one else replace her. During her lunch breaks, she would simply have a sign that she would return after an hour. She was always punctual, not being a minute late. I watched her closely, too. There were only several students who were actively reading at The Hay. I was the outlier and must have appeared like a lunatic to Millie. She knew exactly what I was searching for, yet she made no effort to try to find it. I also didn't want to arouse her suspicion and have her inquire into my identity, so I maintained my low profile.

It was on my fourteenth day at The Hay when I struck gold. It was fortuitous, really. While browsing the general philosophy section, I came across a very nondescript manuscript. It didn't have a proper binding or exterior designation, as Millie suggested it would. It could've been anything. I wouldn't have glanced at it had it not been for the fact that I was looking at anything and everything. I had never had a keen sense of smell, but I when I opened the manuscript, the waft of an extraordinarily strange aroma hit me. I hadn't smelled anything like it. It was so pungent. I looked around to see if any of the students in the library had smelled this extraordinarily strong scent, but they were busy reading.

I slowly opened the manuscript, whose papers had yellowed. It was titled, *"Élan Vital: A Study in Life Unexplained."* The papers had Nadia's original handwriting instead of the standard typewritten text. The entire work looked like a child's art project. There were not only writings but images of indistinct objects, polaroid photos, symbols, and much more. Whoever had compiled this had wanted to capture the entirety of Nadia's last days. This was not a publishable, scientific monograph. It really was more like a diary, an autobiography, with personal depictions that were important to Nadia at that moment. I could not hope to learn anything meaningful by reading this manuscript at The Hay. Instinctively and spontaneously, I ripped out all the pages of the manuscript and placed it into a binder that I kept with me. I looked around to see if anyone was watching before I did this, but Millie was busy reading another Highsmith novel, *The Tremor of Forgery*, and the other students were hard at work. In case any suspicions arose and because I was afraid the manuscript would have a sensor on it, I also decided to return the empty manuscript to the original collections area. At last, I had found what I was looking for. I slipped out inconspicuously just as the library was about to close. I would not return.

NADIA SULLIVAN,
ÉLAN VITAL:
A STUDY IN LIFE UNEXPLAINED **(EXCERPTS)**

My cancer progressed, slower than either my doctor or I expected. I was still coughing up blood and losing weight, but my oxygen level was holding steady. However, my weight was increasing more significantly. Despite the weight loss that the cancer had caused, I had gained approximately fifty pounds. My body had become disproportionately grotesque, but Vincent continued to look at me through his window. I assumed whatever entity had made me conceive was also ensuring that I lived long enough to bear child. I, thus, concluded that the day of my death would coincide with the birth of my child. That is the only way that I could make sense of outliving this malignancy.

Knowing that I could not give birth alone, I hired a midwife to ensure that my delivery would go smoothly. She was a quiet, Muslim woman in her late 60s who spoke no English. Her name was Nasreen. At the time, this is exactly what I needed. I did not desire to converse with anyone. I did not need a friend. I just wanted to guarantee this birth would be successful, that the child would have a chance in this world. If the birth were unscathed, the more important question was who would rear the infant. I had no relatives anywhere. My father had been an only child and, as far as I knew, he had no family with whom he was close, either in the United States or Ireland. I could have certainly placed the child for adoption, but where would I start, I who was losing a little bit more energy every day and, besides that, now experiencing unexplained numbness and weakness in my limbs? Nasreen did not seem even slightly interested in rearing a child. She would eye my abdomen strangely, as if it were securing a devil's child. I could tell that she wanted to ask me about the identity of the fetus's father. But she was afraid of the answer. She dared not ask the question for whose answer she was not ready.

Vincent was still gazing at me every night, as if I were still beautiful, still desired. His piercing looks were somehow sustaining me. Although this could not be scientifically explained, Vincent was this child's father. That I knew. In some universe, he had had intercourse with me, but his progeny had been conceived on this earth. I hearkened to the Buddhist texts, the Greek myths and philosophy and the Indian stories to rid myself of all doubt that this could not be. It was! I had been impregnated. I was bearing child. And I was proof that science could not answer everything, that there was a realm that was outside of its control. I was proof of its partial failure. I recognized the irony of this situation. I, a neuroscientist, on the verge of death, grappling with the failures of science itself while giving birth to a child who had been conceived supernaturally. I was undoubtedly being mocked by Allah. I had been tested by Him and had emerged a failure. I was a harlot, and this child was the byproduct of my darker, sinful nature. If, or when, I gave birth, I assumed that I would die. That was just a thought. Readers will know the answer if I manage to finish this manuscript.

Still experiencing numbness and weakness in my arms, I decided to see my internist one last time before my delivery. I must say that Dr. Kim was still puzzled that my pregnancy was viable. She took my vitals, all of which were normal except my significantly elevated blood pressure. She was concerned that I might develop eclampsia during childbirth. As such, she decided to also send for a blood panel to include genetic disorders of abnormal clotting, such as Factor V Leiden. She was an extremely intelligent physician, and her age had provided her with much wisdom. My intuition told me that I had a clotting disorder of some kind. How else could I explain these other symptoms? But, even if I were treated for this condition, I did not hope to make it. Either this coagulopathy or this cancer would kill me. I decided to take my chances and let the die be cast. Alea iacta est. Suetonius is to have said this to Julius Caesar, as he led his army across the Rubicon River in Northern Italy. Although we lived in different periods, my fate was no different from these historical characters'. We had each passed a period of no return. There was no turning back.

Feeling unwell for the latter part of the week and realizing that the child would be born within a week, I decided to write a short note to Vincent and let him know of my decision to leave the child with him to rear. Was I thinking about my future death? Was I imagining it? No, I had far greater concerns. I was concerned about the life of this child, the one who would be brought into the world miraculously, without a mother to fend for it. I also did not even think about the consequences of my actions, the questions that Vincent would ask, the decisions he would make, the utter chaos that would enter his world. I knew none of those answers, although I knew that Vincent was the child's proper father. He had observed the stages of my pregnancy, so he would be prepared for a child. He would make a good father, I thought. Without a wife, without children of his own, this child could be his entry into a different world. In case I died in childbirth, of which I was certain, I gave instructions to Nasreen to take the new-born infant to Vincent's doorstep, ring the doorbell, and leave the infant with the curt note below.

"Dear Vincent, if you have received this note, know that I have passed away. Please take care of this child as if it were your own because, in some ways, it is. I think you know this already."

Icould not have anticipated what I would read or see in Nadia's manuscript. It was a new world to me, one that I could palpably feel, as if I were Nadia herself. Her monastic and lonely life, her diagnosis with cancer, her battle with the tenets of Islam, all of it was so heartbreakingly genuine. I could see her living her last days in her bedroom, guilt-ridden and anxious for what would befall her next. But the part about her copulation with her next-door neighbor, Vincent, was simply astonishing. Was this something I could believe? Her story was so credible up to that point, but the part about the levitation and the spiritual intercourse was baffling and came out of nowhere. Had she possibly become delusional and mad prior to her delivery? Had she concocted a double of herself, a doppelgänger, to do her dark bidding? What was that shadow to which she was referring? Was that an actual person lurking around her home? I'm a spiritualist and I do believe in spirits, but this revelation of her as an impregnated Virgin Mary was just too improbable to consume. Nadia was diagnosed with a clotting disorder prior to giving birth. When she died, could this have been the reason? What in her writings were relevant to me? Was she trying to draw a comparison between her death and Catherine's? Did Catherine also have a clotting disorder that killed her while she gave birth? Is that why she perished? That is the only logical conclusion I could draw, which had significance for me. There were so many questions, but no one to decipher these little puzzles for me. The more I read, the more entangled I became in her story and her reason to remain a spirit, so she could offer a message.

It was only when I started to look at the strange images and polaroid photos in her book that I began to see the emergence of a pattern. Her precise handwriting in the first few chapters had been transformed into something nebulous and chaotic, to the point where I could not even make out some of the words. There were photos of images of lights, some diaphanous, some brightly colored. One Polaroid photo looked very distinctly like a man's shadow. Were these of the spirits—Vincent's or others'—that she was attempting to photograph? There were no explanations. Then there were illustrations of her naked body, her legs splayed, with vagina and pubic hair, all on display. If I didn't know better, I would think she was possessed by the devil. The transformation from the beginning to the end of the manuscript was so stark. She was certainly traumatized. But by what? By spirits? No, I had experienced real trauma to know this was something physical, something corporeal and tangible.

Her text was telling me something, but what? I would probably have to read between the lines. Hadn't she told me in our session that one always doesn't need eyes to see? That sentence had stood out to me conspicuously, as if that was the key to my conundrum.

What did that mean, exactly? Her manuscript was replete with images, so this piece of her advice was contrary to the images in her text. Could she have meant that I should look for things that I would expect to be in her manuscript but weren't? This assertion was more plausible, but what was that missing element? I then realized that although Vincent figured very prominently in Nadia's story, he really was a missing figure. He was a mysterious character about whom I knew nothing. My next step was to contact him.

As I was not adept at the world wide web or the internet, as they called it, I consulted the phone book to see if I could find Vincent Duchene's contact number. Luckily, his name was in the white pages, and, as expected, his home was the one listed next to Nadia's old home and now mine. I hadn't seen anyone enter and exit that home, so I assumed that Vincent no longer lived there. I decided to call the number to verify this before I physically visited it. My appearance wasn't exactly welcoming.

"Hello," the person on the other end said. It was a woman's voice. She sounded young, even childish. "Can I speak with Mr. Vincent Duchene, please?" I said, rather nonchalantly. "Who is this?" she replied. "I'm an old friend of his from medical school," I lied. "I'm afraid he no longer lives here. He passed away years ago," the woman replied. I tried to sound compassionate. "Oh, I'm so sorry to hear that. Please accept my condolences. Are you related to him?" I ventured, realizing this question was probably not appropriate so quickly under the circumstances. "No, he was a friend of my mother's, but I knew him well. We were sad to see him go so soon," she said. I took another gamble by replying, "I know he had a child. Do you know where I can find them?" At this, she hesitated. Had I gone too far in asking this? Would she think I was a creep who was trying to extract information to which I was not privy? However, she had just stopped to reassess everything. "He had two daughters, twins to be exact. They've moved away since. I wish I could give you more information, but we lost touch. Goodbye." And just like that, and with this new information, everything was made both clear and opaque. Two daughters? Twins? Nadia's manuscript had mentioned one child. Could Vincent have adopted another? How could he? The woman on the phone had mentioned the two girls were twins. How old would they be now? I calculated them to be around twenty-six years of age. Duchene was a not a very common name. It shouldn't be too difficult to decipher where they lived.

I looked through the white pages again, but this time I was unsuccessful. Obviously, it would have been much easier if I could speak with Vincent, but he was dead. I wondered who his children were. At this point, they would have graduated from college, assuming they went that route. Did I even know if they lived in Providence or the surrounding areas? Of course not, but I had no choice. I had to start somewhere.

I ventured to see if the Web had any clues to offer me. I typed in Duchene and saw a litany of references to Guillaume Duchenne, a renowned French neurologist. His name, with an extra "n," was immortalized in muscular dystrophy, as in Duchenne's muscular dystrophy. Could he and Vincent be related in some way? Perhaps, he was Vincent's grandfather. That was certainly a possibility, given that Vincent was also a physician. Did this have any significance? At that moment, I just desired to know if I could find Vincent's daughters. I typed in Duchene and

Providence as the key words and finally found something that could be valuable. An obituary in the Providence Daily announced that a woman whose name was Mallory Duchene had recently died of an "unfortunate accident." What could that be? Apparently, she had a twin sister, Morgan. I vowed that I would exhaust all possibilities. Morgan was my last chance.

THE MAN

I was getting better at navigating the Web. I typed in Morgan Duchene's name and, instantaneously, found her name on the roster of ER residents at Massachusetts Hospital. She should be easy to track down, I thought. I tried to call the hospital to learn if she was there, but the hospital operator couldn't provide me any more information. "Yes, Dr. Duchene is a resident here, and if you'd like to contact her, you can page her," she said. "But I don't have the number of her pager, or I would've done that myself," I replied harshly. "I'm sorry," she responded, "You may have better luck if you come to the hospital, then." She was as helpful as that librarian at The Hay.

I decided to take the train from Providence to Boston, which was short of an hour. I took the Amtrak Northeast Regional from Providence Station at 1:05 pm, which took me to Boston's South Station at 1:50 pm. From there, I took a taxi to the Hospital, at Boston's East End Neighborhood. I hadn't been to Boston for quite some time and felt the hustle and bustle of the city this time. Perhaps, it was because of the relative isolation I had felt in the past week, but I felt assaulted from the city's cacophony. I was bombarded by the traffic, by taxi drivers who yelled obscenities at the pedestrians: "Get the fuck out of the street!" "Go fuck yourself, man." Boston hadn't changed. But I had. During the interim since I was here, I had butchered my wife, and dumped her and little Emma's corpse in a lake in California. I had conversed with a spirit and found a manuscript, which meant everything or nothing. In short, I was a mess, and it showed.

I entered the imposing and frenetic hospital from its main entrance. I immediately stood out against the white coats of the residents and doctors, and the normal looking people who inhabited the lobby. Apparently, I was still a freak. The people's gazes revealed that. I went up to the registration desk. An affable, elderly man, who had a volunteer pin on his uniform, cordially greeted me. "I'm looking for one of the ER residents, Morgan Duchene, who works here. I'm a family member. Do you know where I can find her?" He appeared to be genuinely helpful. Looking at his screen, he became worried and replied, "Yes, she's here, but I'm afraid she's hospitalized in the step-down unit of the hospital. I'm so sorry to tell you this." I was taken aback. I hadn't expected this complication. Yet another roadblock. "Oh, my," I said, trying to sound concerned, although I was not a good actor. "Is it critical?" as I tried to make my voice go an octave higher. "Well, the step-down unit, or the SDU as we call it, is a step between the ICU and regular rooms, which implies she is getting better. I don't have any more information. But she's on the eleventh floor in room 1145 if you'd like to talk to her nurse." "Yes, that'd be great," I immediately responded, trying to retreat before he asked me any more questions about my identity. He gave me a name badge. He told me to write my name down on it and wear it. I told him I would. I never did. "Thanks. You've been very helpful," I concluded. "You're welcome. I hope she recovers quickly," he replied.

I took the lift to the eleventh floor, which was replete with more white coats and chatter among the residents and doctors. Some coats were long and some short. I assumed it had to do with seniority. I felt looks from all sides, but I kept my gaze down before I disembarked on the eleventh floor. I slowly walked to Morgan's room, where I was greeted by another affable health care worker. I was starting to like this hospital. "Hi, I'm Dr. Duchene's nurse. Can I help you?" she said. "Hi, I'm Morgan's uncle. I heard about her unfortunate accident. I want to see her if that's possible." "Thank god," she replied. "We've been trying to contact her family members, but it appears that no one is listed in her contact information. Here, let's go and see if she's awake. She'll be glad to see you." This was a little too fast for me. I wanted to gauge the situation before I went to see Morgan. "Oh," I exclaimed, "is Morgan awake?" "She's what we call semi-lucid," the nurse said, "which means she veers in and out of consciousness. But she's not in a coma, if that's what you're asking. Come on. Let's go see her together. She'll be delighted to see a relative." I figured I had nothing to lose. If Morgan didn't recognize me, I'd chalk it up to her delirium. "O.K.," I said.

In entering the room, I saw a woman, probably in her mid-20s, with short, jet-black hair who was quite thin. She looked emaciated and not very healthy-looking. She didn't strike me as being a resident, from the many I had recently seen in the lobby and elevator. Nevertheless, I went up to her and said, "Morgan, it's uncle. Do you know who I am? I can't believe this happened to you," although I didn't know what had truly led to her hospitalization. The nurse nicely interjected: "Dr. Duchene is actually very lucky. She had us all a little worried. She had a flurry of seizures, which completely debilitated her for a week. We had to briefly place her in what we call a medically induced coma, so that her brain could slow down and heal. As you may know from the newspapers and TV channels, the hospital has been in a bit of turmoil recently with the patient who came and made a whole lot of people sick here. Unfortunately, Dr. Duchene was in the epicenter of it all and got the brunt of the damage. We think she's recovering well, though. She may be a little sleepy now, but if you'd like, you can wait thirty minutes or so to see if she wakes up." "I think I'll do that," I replied. "Thanks so much for your assistance." "You're very welcome," she replied.

With the nurse out of the room, I looked at Morgan more closely. Her hospital gown was in disarray and had hiked up to her thighs. She was actually very beautiful in a rugged and disheveled way. But you could also tell that she was a rebel. Her short jet-black hair and a small tattoo of a purple flower—perhaps a magnolia—on her right inner thigh relayed a bit about her personality. She had a prominent vein near her hairline, which was not very pleasant to look at. She could cover that with her hair, I thought. Could she be the product of a virgin birth? The thought itself was ridiculous, but I entertained it, nonetheless.

I ventured to talk to her to see if she would respond. "Morgan, Morgan, can you hear me?" Her eyes opened for a second and closed again. Apparently, she had just been administered her anti-seizure medication and a shot of morphine, so she was drowsy. "I'm here to talk to you about your mother, Nadia Sullivan. You have never met her, but she wanted to let you know that she will be communicating with you. I realize that it sounds insane, but I'm a spiritualist and talked to her spirit." As I was saying this, I realized that any person would think this was a jest. It sounded ridiculous coming from my mouth. Morgan then opened her mouth, with her eyes still closed and said, "Cherry, is that you? What are you saying to me? Who's Nadia Sullivan?" I realized she was probably delirious but tried again. "I read your mother's book, and it says that you may have a genetic blood disorder, Factor V Leiden deficiency. It seems that your mother died while giving birth from this disorder. She was concerned about you. Please heed her warning. I don't know if you're registering any of this." With her eyes still closed, she said, "Cherry, I hear you. Let's get away. Are you really my mother? I have a blood disorder?" Clearly, Morgan's delirium was getting worse, so I decided to return once she was more lucid. "Morgan, I'm going now. Just remember that your mother, Nadia Sullivan, is looking out for you. She'll protect you." "Don't leave me, Cherry. Don't leave me, Mother," she said. Morgan became agitated and the sensors started beeping, at which time I decided to leave.

"How was she?" her nurse asked when I left the room. "I'm afraid she's still delirious from all the drugs. I'll return later," I said. "Those drugs can do that to you. Well, I'm sure Dr. Duchene will appreciate your return. Bye, now," she cordially replied. "By the way," I asked her before I left, "who is this Cherry to whom Morgan refers?" "Yes, she seems fixated on that Cherry, doesn't she?" she replied. "Cherry is the infamous patient whose bodily fumes caused all sorts of havoc in the hospital. That's when Morgan began to have these seizures that hospitalized her. I'm surprised you haven't heard of her," she said. "Oh, I have," I lied, "I just didn't know her name." The nurse responded, "Well, interestingly, Cherry, too, is now being kept on this floor. The entire thing has been surreal, to say the least. I think she's in room 1111, although you would probably have to wear a Hazmat suit and a CM-7M gas mask, not that you'd do that. We've had a seriously bizarre couple of weeks here at this hospital. I mean super, super bizarre." "Well, thanks for all that information," I told her, and left.

I decided to walk toward Cherry's room and see what the commotion was about. The closer I reached her room I felt a spirit not dissimilar to the one that I had sensed when I had entered the Crucifix home: Nadia's spirit. Could Cherry be a transmogrification of Nadia? At a certain point, I was not allowed to come closer. There were scientists all over the place, entering and exiting her room. I wondered whether I knew any of them and if they would recognize me, but I assumed they were all from New England. Nadia's spirit was hovering in this hospital. There was no doubt about it. But what she wanted was anyone's guess.

A few days later when I returned to the hospital to speak with Morgan, I was told she was discharged. I was absolutely flabbergasted when they told me where they had taken her. What had caused this to transpire? I would shortly find out from the newspaper and TV channels.

Part V
VINCENT
& MORGAN

Cold is the night. Vincent awakens to a din. It is around 3 a.m. His silent quarters have turned into such a loud reverberation. He reflexively stops his ears with his index fingers. He momentarily thinks of Odysseus's men who were given bees' wax to prevent themselves from hearing the Sirens' song. Odysseus was tied to the ship's mast. Although Odysseus heard the mellifluous tune, he couldn't be drawn to the island of those temptresses. He was wisely bound to that mast. Vincent recognizes that Nadia is his temptress. She is the siren who has lured him into her dark history. Or maybe he has drawn her into his. She never asked to be surveyed. She never asked to be an unknowing confidant of a dying man. Or did she? He may have been played all along.

The clangor continues. It's neither melodious nor alluring, like the Siren's singing, yet he is drawn to its mysterious source. His bed is now in the sitting room. He realizes that he is too weak to continue to move from his bedroom to this room. Nadia is now continually in his thoughts. It makes sense to have her as close to him as possible. She has him so mesmerized. Vincent arises from his bed, listless and drained. He heads to the window. He gazes out of it. This window has become his only avenue of escape. He sees the world through this transparent theater. It is world that contains Nadia within it. He has had no desire to leave these quarters and venture outside. He is content here, watching Nadia. He is content realizing that he has someone else to die with him.

The lace curtains covering Nadia's window still partially conceal the theater within. However, he makes out two shadowy figures. One is Nadia. He notices her disheveled hair. He glimpses what appear to be her dark, hard eyes. They are the eyes of a viper now. Cold, elliptical, and opaque. They are the eyes of an animal that is preparing for an attack. Nadia's frenetic energy is evident. She is trying to reason with a towering shadow who hovers over her, who dwarfs her. The midwife that Nadia has hired for this birth is not present. The shadow has taken the midwife's place. Vincent wonders if this could be the child's father. He judges the height of this shadow at six feet, his own height. Nadia gesticulates. Her facial features suggest that she is angry, that something or someone has perturbed her. She is throwing items at the Figure. She is vehemently arguing with him. Her body moves to and fro. It appears to be vibrating, like a hummingbird's wing. Is he hallucinating a bad dream? Is he still confused because of an abrupt arousal from sleep? Is this reality? Nadia's body appears to be levitating. Vincent is clearly confused, he thinks. He returns to bed and conjures this episode to a hallucination that arose from his sleep. In an instant, he falls asleep.

Although physically alive, I was dead inside. Throughout all my medical interventions, Cherry was at my side. I felt connected to her in a way that I wasn't to anyone else. I had only interacted with her for a few hours in the ER, but I felt we knew each other like we were sisters. She prodded me on. She served as my cheerleader. Perhaps, she was my guardian angel, my dead sister coming to heal me. I don't know. I won't know. How else can I explain it to you? I've never really believed in anything of the sort, the spiritual, the occult, what have you, but this was different. It was as if I were in a dream, or under ether, but Cherry was truly talking to me at the side of my hospital bed. It was reality, hypersimulated. I was under considerable morphine. A few of my colleagues had mentioned to me that I was hallucinating, that I was speaking with another person who wasn't there. Perhaps. I would veer into and out of their conversations. I was so drugged. But I could see Cherry, perhaps in a hallucination or not. She was now more presentable with clean face. She had no smudged red lipstick or black eyeliner. She looked beautiful in all her simplicity. We had met several more times in this hospital room, but this was the encounter that I remembered most vividly.

We spoke about my dead sister's tragic accident, my father, and the mother I didn't know. When I mentioned my mother, Cherry became distraught and saddened. I even saw her crying a little. "What's wrong, Cherry?" I remember asking her. "What has upset you?" She answered in her usual soft and robotic manner, "It's nothing. I remember my own mother who died in the hospital before giving birth to me. You know, I experienced it. All of it, the birth and all." I didn't know how to react. Clearly, this was becoming more of a hallucination than an actual encounter. Cherry continued: "I know you'll have a difficult time believing this. Spiritually, I am your mother, in a different woman's body, a body that has already outlived its years and is decaying." I looked at her aghast. I gazed at Cherry's quivering, dry lips and the way she enunciated her words, as if this were the truth. She continued: "That is the reason that no one can save me. I'm already decomposing. I'm already dying. The noxious smell that made you sick is the putrefaction of my corpse. The shiny sheen on my skin is my body's attempt to save itself. I know it's implausible. It seems like a prank, doesn't it? Believe what you want. This is me. This is the truth." I remained incredulous, in my dreams or whatever this reality was. I wasn't sure anymore. But at that moment, I had so many questions to ask my presumed mother. "What's my mother's name, Cherry?" I inquired. She thought about this for a few seconds, stared at me directly, and said, "Nadia Sullivan." She then continued, with the voice of another. It was a voice that was much deeper, sadder, and nostalgic. "I gave birth to you and your sister before I died." "Listen to me carefully," she calmly and slowly said, "You have a genetic disorder. Your grandmother died from it while giving birth to me. I died, too, while giving birth to you and your sister. If you choose to give birth, you, too, will perish. That is the message I wanted to deliver. And, of course, to see you." I then felt Cherry's oily and garlic-tasting lips on my own. We kissed for a while, as if we were in love and she was my girl. She then said, "I love you, child. I'll do my best, as always, to protect you. You lost your sister much too early. We won't let that happen to you, too." Then, as if my dream had ended, she vanished. I looked around. She was nowhere to be found. At that moment, all the monitors set off alarming sounds. My heart was advancing into ventricular tachycardia. I was fighting for my life again, with that bastard Death one step behind me.

My heart briefly veered into a dark zone before it was shocked again to reality. The last thing I recall before it was resuscitated was my conversation with Cherry. I questioned whether any of this was real. Delirium in an ICU setting was not uncommon. But my encounter with Cherry or Nadia or whoever was more vivid and palpable than anything I had previously encountered. I gathered that Cherry was still alive. My colleagues were speaking about her. The hospital was still deeply immersed in her case. I could see scientists and doctors, donned in Hazmat suits, enter and exit her room. I needed to see Cherry before she physically expired. Like she had told me, her body was rotting away with every minute.

During those days, I was still weak and could barely get up to brush my teeth in a cup, my makeshift basin. I breathed, ate, and shat, but I considered myself good as dead. Nothing moved me anymore. Nothing came close to the exhilaration that I felt with Cherry, the way she and I had taunted Death during our encounters, along this unknown precipice, this strange, otherworldly border. I couldn't think of anything or anyone else. I could still see her shiny, glowing skin. I could smell her. I could taste her aroma of vinegar and garlic on my lips. Who was she, really? Who was I, after our encounter, after this was all over? What remained? What mattered? But was this over? Was that all there was?

I was under the gun again, with Death pointing its gun at my head. *It's you or her, or both,* it said. *One or both of you will go. One or both of you will die. I'm too old for this kind of shit,* it continued to say. *You've become a pest to me lately.* But you know what? I enjoyed it this time. In our own perverted way, Cherry and I were Thelma & Louise, in total control of what we both needed, even if that meant self-destruction, even if that meant flying off the cliff to save our fucking lives, even if that meant true annihilation. Although in free fall, we knew exactly where we were headed, a place where Death would have no control over us. In this new space where we conversed together, we had found a haven, our own Shangri-La, days of roses and Heaven. We had left the nights of thorns and Hell behind us.

Each day, Vincent is gaining more weight. Each day, Nadia is losing weight. Vincent's cheeks become rosier, while Nadia's complexion becomes more jaundiced. Life begins to grow inside of him, while death continues to grow within her more forcefully than before. It's an interesting turn of events. Vincent now looks to Nadia with pity. He wonders what has created this imbalance. They are no longer mirrors of one another. Their images are distorted. Her blackened nipples have receded in size. They no longer remind him of his dead wife's eyes. They now resemble black holes through which Nadia will disintegrate soon. They now just signify a remnant of who she once was, months ago.

Nadia's eyes have also lost their glimmer. They are not as fierce as they once were. In them, Vincent cannot glimpse that tenacity which endeared her to her own existence, however precarious that may have been. It appears that Vincent is deriving Nadia's nutrients at her expense. He has become an unknowing parasite. He is benefiting from her bare existence. She still does not look outside her window to see if someone is scrutinizing her. Perhaps she realizes that she doesn't want to elicit pity from others. Perhaps she is too broken. Perhaps she is just too resigned for her future death.

Vincent has made love to Nadia from a distance on numerous occasions. He has caressed her breast and black nipples; he has kissed her dry and chafing lips. He has entered and impregnated her. It's plausible that he has taken so much of her for himself that she is now no longer who she once was. He has taken so much that she no longer has much to give. But is he sure that he has only copulated with her from a distance? No, once he took Nadia's body unwillingly. He drugged her. He chained Nadia's legs and arms to her bed and entered her. His desire was simply too strong. There is a place that Vincent likes to go in his head, up above. It's a place where he sees others in their little ways. It's a place that he's ashamed of. It's a place where he goes when he's lonely.

Still seriously ill, I disconnected the oxygen sensor from my finger and the EKG leads from my chest. I then changed from my hospital gown to some old scrubs that I had in a plastic bag when I was transferred here from the ICU. I told my nurse that I needed a break. She understood and excused herself. Shift change was my opportunity. It was during shift change when nurses transfer their patients' notes. It's a time of chaos. I knew this would be my only opportunity to see Cherry again. I combed my disheveled hair and tried to look tidy, as if I were a working resident. I also donned a surgical mask to ensure at least a basic level of anonymity. I had been transferred from the ICU to the step-down unit. There would be no one who would recognize me here. I opened the door slightly to make sure no nurses were in sight, and then slipped out. At this point, I felt certain that I'd be undetected. The nurses here were not as observant as those in the ICU. I could do this, I thought. I could blend in seamlessly with these healthcare professionals.

I nimbly walked through the halls of the unit, almost sliding on the linoleum floor with my slippers, the only shoes at my disposal. Although I was feeling slightly feverish, the delirium of that heat was exhilarating. It gave me energy. It gave me life. I felt like my old self again, the Morgan who didn't give a shit about anything, the Morgan who was stoned and inebriated half the time. I had Death alongside me now. It was no longer walking behind me. It was at my side, a Bonnie to its Clyde. I needed to know where they had taken Cherry. I desperately needed to know if she was alive, that her body had not decomposed yet.

I entered the nurses' station. With my surgical mask in place, I was unrecognizable here. Nurses and doctors would float in and out, without any surveillance. Although my brain was still foggy, my log-in name and password were etched in my brain like a chisel to wood. The hospital had just purchased a computer system to input orders electronically, so it took me a while to remember the process. Finally, I logged onto the server and was amazed to learn that Cherry, too, had been moved from the ICU to this same floor. It made my job so much easier.

The staff had roomed Cherry in the corner room, in the East corridor of the eleventh floor. Room 1111. My lucky number. Would it be so lucky this time? I was surprised to see the security guards whom I presumed to have been stationed at the entrance to her room were no longer there. I also didn't see any scientists with their Hazmat suits, either. Could Cherry be dead? If so, the patient log probably had not been updated. The thought entered but then exited just as quickly. I needed her alive to ask the questions that were so vital to me.

Surprisingly, the door to her room was open. No nurses were in sight, although I suspected that due to a change in shifts. I entered Cherry's room. She was alone, sitting there. In her usual way, she was looking straight ahead, like an automaton, while acknowledging my presence. "Oh, it's you," she said. She then turned around to face me. I saw Cherry's almost dead eyes look at me. Her big, black eyes looked like a doe's—a doe that is about to get shot. Although her eyes looked drowsy, there was a fluorescent glimmer that was shifting and shining. She recognized me. She knew who I was. I smelled a faint scent of cheap baby shampoo and an old fragrance I recognized from childhood, perhaps. "Cherry, it's me. It's time to wake up. We have to go. You and I can get out of here if we really want. Come on. I have so many questions to ask you. I don't know if I was dreaming it all, but it seemed so real," I told her, without taking a breath. We didn't have much time before we were found out. I had to convince her quickly. What was my plan? I didn't know, but I recognized that Cherry was the answer and that we needed to leave this place.

She arose out of her stupor, magnificently, and spewed forth an enigmatic saying: "People have seen the things I've done. But they're just copies of me, just shadows. I'm not who they think I am. But you've seen me for who I am. Seeing without seeing." She then paused and continued. "Do it. Kill me, Morgan. Do it now," she continued. "What do you mean, Cherry?" I said, horrified by the thought. "Do I look like someone who could hurt you?" I uttered.

"These pain killers are wearing off. I don't have much time. I want you to stop me, Morgan. I'm broken. Don't you understand? I've been broken the moment I was born. I've been lost," Cherry urgently announced. I was at a loss for words. I was at a loss for action. I just stood there looking at Cherry, who now looked perfectly normal, with her hair tied back and her face clean, just as I remembered her during our encounters, perhaps on earth, perhaps in a dream.

At that moment, she could've been in a Cover Girl commercial, so easy, breezy, and simple she looked. She could've been my sister. I thought about Mallory, briefly, and then about Cherry, longer. She could be anyone, yet she was Cherry, a stranger from a different land, a different galaxy, perhaps. I wasn't sure yet. After a few seconds of silence, Cherry spoke again, this time slower, much slower, as if she wanted me to get her message correct. "When I die," she said, "please don't let them bury me in a coffin six feet underground. You see, I have claustrophobia, and even in death, I wouldn't be able to stand it. Instead, cremate me. Expel my ashes in the sea, any sea. I'd like to be like fish and swim in the open, morning air." "But you can't go, Cherry. Please don't go," I replied, emotionally. "So, come," she said. "Come with me to this other world. We'll face the future together." In her vacuously big black eyes, I could see that she was ready to forget this world to become someone else. Later, I would always return to this moment, to this encounter with her, to the memories of my childhood.

This is not the encounter that I had imagined between me and Cherry. She was talking about death, while I was trying to understand how she fit into my life. She had already stopped looking, while I had just begun. I needed to ask her the question that had been percolating in my mind all this time, the question that I was apprehensive in asking. I had to face the truth. "Cherry," I rattled off, "I know this may sound bizarre, but are you my mother? I mean, do you have my mother's soul within you?"

She was silent at first, and then she answered me, plainly, as if she had just landed on earth again after a momentous journey into the galaxy. "Your mother? Where'd you get that crazy shit of an idea? No, I'm Cherry, a bastard from Oklahoma who just wanted a chance to live peacefully and simply on this earth. I'm dying from pain and cancer now. All I ask is that you rid me of this misery. I've lived a life of shit here. I'm dying. I'm fucked-up. Can't you see that? You must let me die, so I can finally live."

Her answer both relieved and distressed me. It made my future simultaneously simpler but hopeless. Her encounter with me in my hospital room was nothing more than an illusion. I had been hoping for a mother, but, instead, I had projected this onto Cherry, the enigmatic protagonist of my narrative.

My contact with her was just simply a projection, what I wanted in a mother I never knew. That was the easiest and most sensible explanation. How could I have believed otherwise? I felt stupid for asking her, but it had all seemed so real. How did I summon Nadia Sullivan's name? It was a bad joke. I felt duped, as if I had read all the signs incorrectly.

No doubt, Cherry was in excruciating pain. I looked at her morphine drip. It was almost empty. I had such little time before the nurse returned. If I hoped to give Cherry some eternal comfort, I couldn't waste time on an IV drip. I went to the nurses' drug closet, input the code that I had memorized so well, and took out five ampules of morphine, each at a dose of 10 mg. I also took several syringes and needles. I ran into her room, mixed the compound with distilled water, and started to inject her intramuscularly. Four of these injections would do the job, I thought. They would kill her painlessly.

Cherry looked at me while I was administering the injections. Her eyes looked like a wounded doe, as it is about to expire. Her last words to me were a simple "Thank you for saving me." She then kissed my neck and must have scraped it with her sharp incisors because I bled a little. I looked at her, overcome with tears and surprise. "You're welcome," I replied. I hadn't retrieved any answers to help me with my own life, but I knew I had served my role as a physician, to heal those who were dying. I had never thought of myself as a doctor before. Everything was so technical for me, but, somehow, Cherry had changed me. I really felt for her. Perhaps this was my life lesson, not anything profound or startling like I had hoped, but something as simple as this, what I had pledged to do since medical school: to heal, to salve pain.

As I was injecting Cherry with the last ampule, I realized that she was a heartbeat away from the hereafter, wherever or whatever that was. A burly nurse briskly and unexpectedly entered the room. I was caught red-handed like a confident thief whose ingenious plans have suddenly gone awry. "What are you doing?" she asked aggressively. At first, she wasn't sure who I was or what I was doing, but then she caught on quickly. Not hesitating, she pushed the emergency alarm and secured the door. By that time, it was too late. Cherry's heart monitor showed a progression to asystole. Her heart stopped. Her breathing ceased. She died.

It happens tonight. Thunder rumbles and cracks. Vincent awakens from sleep. The sound is resonant of a nail being struck, repeatedly, into metal. There is no question about it now. He cannot be imagining this. Not now. Everything is transparent. The lace curtains have been drawn open. Darkness has receded. The window is the centerpiece. A spotlight is being shed on it. It appears as if the show is being performed for Vincent, at his request. Vincent glimpses Nadia. Her arms and legs are chained to her bed. The monstrous figure is hammering chains into it. Nadia is screaming uncontrollably. She is in active labor. She is flailing her limbs in all directions. She cries. She screams. It is the first time the window is open.

The shadow from last night is hovering above her, again. This time, however, Vincent makes out the outline of a face. It is his. He cannot stop looking at this cinematic horror. Nadia continues to scream. It is so very loud. He imagines that it could be as loud as Pasiphae's, as she was giving birth to her son, the Minotaur, that half-man, half-bull. He glimpses the head of a child. Nadia is crowning. From her facial expression, Vincent realizes Nadia is in extreme pain. The midwife prepares to take hold of the infant. The infant's body follows shortly. The midwife uses a sharp object to sever the umbilical cord. The shadow smiles. It has obtained what it desires. The midwife places the infant into an ivory bassinet. There is another bassinet adjoining it. A few minutes later, the face of another infant emerges. Nadia screams, long and low. She cries in pain. Vincent imagines the shining, wet fluid that accompanies the infants. The midwife places this baby into the second bassinet. Nadia continues to scream more forcefully. She drowns the entire world. Vincent is sure he is the only one who hears this deafening howl. He then falls into a vertiginous swoon.

WCVB-TV
ABC-Boston
July 30, 1996

Television Reporter: Good evening. In a complex story that continues to evolve at magnificent speed, there are now more twists. This highly bizarre event, now referred to as Boston's Toxic Summer Storm, has been considered a medical mystery since the beginning. It has led to speculation as to how a patient can infect an entire emergency room with toxic ammonia-like fumes emitting from her body. After numerous interviews, officials initially concluded that the hospital staff, who were primarily women, suffered from a mass hysteria triggered by an odor.

However, more recently, with the expertise of reputable scientists, a potential chemical explanation for this incident has been proposed. The hypothetical scenario depends upon the oxidation of a common solvent, dimethyl sulfoxide to dimethyl sulfate. The latter compound is a highly volatile and highly toxic agent that can be quite hazardous to humans in small amounts. The descriptions of the hospital-staff victims appear quite consistent with dimethyl sulfate exposures.

The woman, whose identity remains unknown, initially presented to Massachusetts Hospital with pelvic pain and profuse vaginal bleeding. She was later diagnosed with late-stage cervical cancer. Sources suggest that she was covering her skin daily with a large quantity of DMSO, or dimethyl sulfone, as a possible way to cure her cancer. DMSO, which had gained popularity as a solution for many types of ailments, was labeled as a toxic substance in 1965. It can be oxidized with oxygen to dimethyl sulfate. This theory suggests that while the patient, who had been rubbing DMSO cream on her body to relieve her pain, was being intubated, the oxygenation transformed that innocuous compound to something lethal and hazardous.

More recently, the story shifts again, this time to the Irish-Italian organized crime gangs in Boston, placing the hospital in the precarious role of one of the largest methamphetamine distribution points in the U. S. This theory suggests that hospital workers were smuggling precursor chemicals in IV bags. Unfortunately, one of these could have been given to the patient described above, which could explain the smell of ammonia and the possible emission of such toxic fumes. An emergency medicine resident at Massachusetts Hospital, Morgan Duchene, appears to be at the center of this maelstrom, having killed the patient who initially presented with her bizarre presentation. We await to see what other theories are put forth in this case that has turned so insanely problematic.

So before they handcuffed me and took me to Bay State Correctional Center, I grabbed and wrapped a razor blade in athletic tape, and hid it in my mouth. Early that morning, it rained. It rained like it had never done before in Boston. I knew those were Cherry's tears for me, for what she couldn't say in words. Mourning rain, I call it. Was I sure this was not the second passing of my mother, too? No, not quite. But I wanted to believe so much. Could it be true what Nadia had told me, in Cherry's body, that I had that genetic blood disorder, like her and her mother before her? That is, if I believed there was a Nadia. It was simple enough to get a blood test. That would sort it out, I thought. What was I saying? Was I delusional? I didn't know about the truth anymore. I didn't know anything. Everything had been thrown off balance. Everything was fucked up.

The coroner's office conduced its autopsy on Cherry's body about a week after she expired. Its plan was straightforward. In addition to examining the deceased organs, as is routine in any autopsy, it planned to analyze compounds, both organic and inorganic, in the blood, bile, and tissue from Cherry's organs: her heart, liver, brain, and kidneys. The team of examiners also planned to check for any gases that may have vented off the samples.

The team was looking for that elusive object it would never find. Each was hoping to solve the puzzle that had frustrated us all. What in Cherry's body exuded that noxious and lethal gas that had almost killed me and made a group of people severely ill? Why was her blood so extraordinary, the likes of which no one had seen? Even in death, Cherry was fireproof, as if her body could not be permeated willingly, as if gases could voluntarily escape it but not enter, as if her heart had been broken so many times that it was now indestructible. That's just the way she was. I knew they would never find the actual answer, that Cherry's corpse would elude them at every turn. There would always be more questions. Her body would always lead to more signifiers, more signs, but no solid answers. Her soul could not be located. Death could never take hold of her. I smiled.

Although I still didn't really know who Cherry was, I knew she wasn't just a woman with cancer who had unfortunately come across some meth compound that mixed with her pain cream. That's what the FBI and the health authorities wanted us to believe. I didn't believe that. My faith in her was so much stronger.

Life flies by. We think we'll live a hell of a long time, so we spend our time talking about shit that, in the end, doesn't matter to us. And by the time we realize we won't live long, it's all over. Time has run out. We're done for. The bell has tolled for us. I never really liked Thornton Wilder's play *Our Town*, but I now realize that what I hated about it was its universal truth. We don't have much time here. That night with Cherry, I dived into the pool, and it was extraordinary. I was hoping to dive back in, but Cherry had disappeared into thin air. Her physical remnant was gone, but her spirit lingered.

You're thinking that there must be a scientific reason for Cherry's death and for what happened to us all that fateful night. That she was not a spirit of my late mother's but that I projected that upon Cherry, because I was now an orphan, because I had lost my twin sister, because I was fucked up. Maybe. All those arguments are valid. I would make them, too, if I were on the other side. But I'm not. I'm on the side of having seen it and experienced this intense reality that overwhelmed me, like a tsunami from the other side. Maybe one day you'll see and experience your own Cherry before the government or whoever decides to take them from you.

I'll cut to the chase because no one likes to hear the technicalities of what occurred after I "killed" Cherry. I guess that's the correct term, although I didn't look at is as killing but as providing someone with a dignified death. In the eyes of the law, I was a killer now, charged with first-degree murder. I probably would do it again if presented with similar circumstances, but I didn't care one way or another. In my eyes and in the view of other physicians in the hospital, I was doing a service. I was doing a job that I had vowed to do. I had saved an imminently dying patient from more misery.

The Boston Police Department arrested me a few hours after Cherry's death. To my surprise, not only was I arrested for murder but also for dealing drugs to residents at the hospital. Although this second charge completely caught me off guard, I somehow wasn't the least surprised that things had unraveled the way they did. Maybe I was living the same type of dream that I had had with Cherry. Maybe this was now my new reality. I could see Death smiling at me, like it knew how these chips would fall. I wanted to give it one last "fuck you" before I saw it again, but I neither had the energy nor the interest. In some ways, Death had lost a confidant and a friend. I would never party with it again. "Take that, asshole," I wanted to say. "You'll be a loner now." But words weren't enough for what had happened that week.

I would later learn that Cherry's death was spectacular in a way that I could not fathom. Before my arraignment, when I had been imprisoned for less than a few days, I was visited by a strange man who, for lack of better words, looked like a monster. His tall stature, elongated limbs, and grotesque face were straight out of a horror film. He could certainly have been one of those character actors, who look and talk a certain way, and are always cast as evil, like in a James Bond film. I couldn't figure him out. The guards didn't announce his name. In my orange jumpsuit and oily hair, I made my way to an individual booth, separated by a translucent screen. There was a dirty phone next to it with graffiti etched on the orange receiver. I had seen all of these in serial crime shows, but I was now experiencing it for the first time. I was a genuine criminal now. This setup validated it. It was a new reality. Like anything repetitive, I assumed that I would become slowly accustomed to it. The disgustingly bland bread and tomato sauce concoction that I was eating these past several days came to mind. Jail food was just as bad as I had imagined.

The man sat down in the chair across from me, looking at me directly before picking up the phone. I picked up the receiver several seconds later. There was silence between us, while we eyed one another for close to a minute. None of us knew what they wanted to say. He finally spoke, calmly and very slowly. "Hi, Morgan. Obviously, you don't know me. I wanted to convey a message to you…" He was silent for a few more seconds before he continued, "from your mother." I looked at him. Was this starting again? The scene that

I had played out with Cherry when I had snuck into her room. Now my answers would flow from this enigmatic character about whom I knew nothing. "Who are you?" I quizzically asked. His reply was quicker this time: "You could say, I'm a friend of your mother's. She wanted me to convey a message to you from a place that remains hidden to me, too." I didn't need to ask more. I knew the answer to my question now.

He was surprised that I didn't wince at what he had just said. "Go on, please," I replied. He continued: "She wanted me to attest to the fact that what she said to you in her physical form at the hospital was true. I don't know the specifics, but she had made a concerted effort to relay that message." He waited for as much time as it would take for me to comprehend this. But I was always ready for it, maybe not here or now, but it was expected. "I appreciate your coming here to tell me this," I told him. I didn't need to say more. He and I understood one another. Undoubtedly, he had experienced something as strange as I had. I didn't need to understand his story to understand mine. Before he left, he turned to me quickly, his shoulders a little higher, and said, "One last thing. You may have not realized this, but you saved me. Well, both you and your mother. Your mother absolved me of any wrongdoing. My wife's death wasn't my fault, after all. I understand that now. She would have died regardless." He left before I had a chance to reply.

During my arraignment, I pled guilty to the murder charge, although equivocally (the Judge wasn't happy), hoping for a lesser sentence. I pled not guilty to dealing drugs, which was the truth. I was a pawn in this chess game of theirs, although I only sold weed and one bag of crystal meth to that loser resident. He was the one who ratted me out. The police and the DA colluded with him. I'm sure some deal was made. The other evidence was circumstantial. It looked like I was becoming a scapegoat for trafficking a compound—methylamine—used in making methamphetamine. I was implicated with the South End Mafia. I'd never heard of them until my arrest. But that is how it works out sometimes. I had learned this the hard way. But did any of this matter anyway?

At the end, I was backed into a fucking corner. There really was no way out. However way you cut it, the government had evidence, tenuous and circumstantial, of my alleged conspiracy and dealings with the South End Mafia. I was not a drug dealer, but they could make it appear like I was. They had charged me with possession and distribution of illicit drugs. They were close to charging me with drug trafficking, too, although that was a harder sell. Whoever had placed that batch of methylamines in my on-call locker knew what they were doing. They had wanted to use my addiction to drugs to their advantage to cover up what could not be known about Cherry. Such information could devastate a nation, a country, a universe. I knew their secret. But, because I had killed Cherry, they could get rid of me for good anyway. They didn't need that petty drug charge. I would be ensconced in a prison cell, silenced, without power to expose their cover-up. But I knew the government's weakness, too. How could I or the man that visited me in prison stand against the behemoth that was the U.S. government? Who would believe us? We were cogs in a wheel.

They cremated Cherry's body several days later and, with it, the evidence that would allow us to extricate ourselves from this mess. I couldn't have killed her because she had already perished. She didn't have a heart. She was non-human. That was the truth that couldn't be revealed. The man who had visited me in prison returned before my arraignment with a document in his hand. "I have Cherry's preliminary autopsy report, which I surreptitiously stole. It will exonerate you from her killing. The proof is here. We'll bring down the government that tried to conceal the truth of her body. We'll bring down the scientific establishment, too. Through her body, Cherry saved you." He smiled before showing it to me.

If we knew how things would end, where our journey would take us, would we make the same decisions? Can we escape our fate, or would something deep within us lead us to the same destination? Do we have to let some things go before they find their way back to us? Is everything interconnected? I think a lot about these questions while awaiting trial, while awaiting Cherry's return, in-between time. I know that she'll save me. My story really begins here, at the end, where I've always been.

Dearest You,

Besides the *Demeter Kitten Fur*, another hallucinatory scent of yours haunts me. It, too, was brief. It, too, was unlike you. How do I explain it? That what I remember most about you was nothing that ever resembled you. Always brief. Always cheap. I remember the scent of your hair the last time I smelled it when you were alive. We were eighteen, right before Father's death, before we became estranged from one another. You had just washed your hair with Johnson & Johnson's baby shampoo because Paul Mitchell's *Tea Tree shampoo*—your favorite—-was out. You had stepped out of the shower when your glorious blonde hair just scraped my face. I lost my footing. This was not you. You tousled your hair with the towel and left the bathroom. "The bathroom's all yours, Morgan," you said. The smell of that baby shampoo lingered, as I then thought about our birth, about our childhood. I'm waiting for you, again. I lost you in fires once, but I know that you returned as my Cherry. I initially missed all the signs. The cheap drugstore perfume, the baby shampoo. You were generously providing me with all the signs, with all these clues, but I was focused on who you were to others and not on who you were to yourself. I was also focused on the return of a mother I never knew. Maybe she and you were the same person. I don't know anymore. You left me one minute and then reappeared several minutes later, as someone completely different. I tried to save you a second time by killing you. But I saved you only to see you disintegrate again, right before me. You were correct. You were never meant for this world that you occupied so briefly. Whoever you were—Mallory, Char, Cherry, Mother—you were never you. I could never grasp you; that's why your body was decomposing. You never wanted me to find you, even though you returned a second time. But last night, in this prison cell, I fortuitously found you. You came to me as a furious Angel, an Angel who was unlawfully taken from here. An Angel, so hard, but of the softest kind. In a few seconds, your anger turned to genuine warmth. You smiled at me, hinting that I must be brave enough to follow you. In your own language, you gently said, "So, come." I only understood because you motioned me to follow you, not only with your language but also with that small mark you had made on my neck. And, so, with the small hidden razor blade at my disposal I went with you. I said I would wait, but I just couldn't. Your corpse couldn't save me anymore. Your final autopsy report showed that you had a heart. You loved me, after all.

xx,

Me

I heard the unfortunate news about Morgan from both the newspapers and television channels. She had become a news sensation by killing a patient at the hospital. I didn't know what to believe, but I knew that Mallory had been framed. That's the only way I can explain it. I had been closely following my daughters' lives since I reluctantly left them in front of Vincent's door twenty-six years ago. I was so proud of them. They had excelled more than I could have anticipated. Both had grown up to be such wonderful and strong women, one a doctor and the other a genuine humanitarian. They were intelligent, unselfish, and self-sacrificing. I was utterly devastated by Mallory's death, though. It's taking me a while to recover from that. I'm still feeling those melancholic pangs. I read Mallory's obituary in the Providence Daily, which I had continued to read on a regular basis since I left Providence, fearing the day when I would see their names there one day. I always had a premonition that something unfortunate would happen to my daughters. The past and my family history served as an ominous foreshadowing.

At this point, you are wondering why I vanished and left my daughters in front of someone's door whom I barely knew. No doubt, you're also wondering why I didn't die of that lethal cancer that plagued me. Or how I gave birth to twins when I had expected only one child. I'll answer your questions to the best of my recollection. My memory seems to have faded with time, although I'm grateful that I have not yet been diagnosed with Alzheimer's disease, the ailment to which I had always feared succumbing.

Let's start with the birth. I was surprised that I didn't die through that horrendous turmoil. I had lost a great deal of blood, but the births were successful. Nasreen, the midwife, was adept at her duties and she executed everything perfectly. Dr. Kim had not mentioned that I would be having twins, so you could imagine my shock when Nasreen announced my second child's delivery: "Ms. Sullivan," she said, as I was exerting all my strength to push, "there is another child." I couldn't register it at that moment, especially with my heavy bleeding, but, later, I was in disbelief. The diagnostic ultrasound may not have been accurate in detecting the twins given the edema from my cancer. I was shocked to say the least, but I was hopeful that these twin sisters would at least have each other to protect them.

After their birth and my survival, how could I rear daughters and explain to them that they had no father, that they were products of a miraculous birth? They would think I was deranged. How could I care for them when I was slowly dying of cancer? I had to disappear and make it appear like I had died. Death wouldn't be so far away. That was the only way I could deter Vincent from finding my whereabouts and my daughters from inquiring and searching for me. My death would make that so much easier. I had fled before from the clutches of my father, and I could do so again from this calamity. I instructed Nasreen to carry out this wonderful plan. I forged some medical documents showing that I had died. The monograph that I had written would also bolster the case that I had died of cancer. Death by paper. I even had Nasreen place artificial ashes in a vase to show that I had been cremated in case there were any questions about the legitimacy of my death. I had given her power of attorney, which did not seem implausible given that I had no family members. I established a trust in which I placed some of my assets, including my home. I hadn't planned on selling the house but designated Nasreen as my trustee in case I needed to sell it for money before I died. I withdrew whatever savings I had, which was a nice sum, and left for Stowe, Vermont, to live my last days there. Why Stowe? It seemed like a perfectly small and bucolic town where I could slowly disappear and vanish into the shadows. From that point on, as I was concerned, Nadia Sullivan had died. From her ashes, Mariam Jones would emerge. She would be my new alias.

Over the next few months, I felt more refreshed and alive than I had for a long time. I could not believe that I was still living, that I had lungs to breathe! I attributed this to the scenery and fresh air of Stowe. I also noticed that I was no longer coughing up blood. This change in my disposition was quite unexpected. I decided to establish care with a well-regarded oncologist at the University of Vermont Medical Center. A CT scan of my lungs revealed that, although I still had remnants of cancer, the malignancy had significantly regressed in size. The oncologist advised me to undergo chemotherapy and radiation, which would offer me that assurance that the cancer would not enlarge in size and possibly remit. I reluctantly agreed, although I couldn't believe what had transpired in this short time since I gave birth. Six months later and, on my follow-up and to my mixed delight and disbelief, the cancer was no longer present. How could I explain this? I couldn't, just like I couldn't explain my conception. I had defied the odds, once again. But what would I do now? I had feigned my death and left my daughters under the care of someone whom I barely knew. I could not return to Providence. In an unexpected turn of events, that chapter of my life had involuntarily closed. I could not resurrect Nadia Sullivan even if I wanted to.

I decided to live my remaining years in this small, rustic town of Stowe, with its many hiking trails and cascading waterfalls, and carry out my research as I had done previously. It is true that I no longer had the resources that I had had as a professor at Brown, but I was resourceful and did what I could. I purchased a microscope. I also purchased tiny pigs from the many farms here in Stowe. I dissected their brains. I delved into theory. I devoted the rest of my life to research into the deranged and decomposing brains of pigs. In this way, I passed my days. I was now living under the name of Mariam Jones, keeping a very low profile, not associating with anyone. It was an austere and lonely life. I shorn my long, beautiful black locks and donned a pixie-cut, like a boy's. I dyed my hair a dirty blonde in case any of my previous students or colleagues stumbled upon me. I threw out my hijab with the rest of my clothes. I bought flannel shirts and regular slacks and jeans. I metaphorically killed Nadia and buried her bones. In her stead, I resurrected Mariam Jones from Nadia's ashes. I knew the chance that anyone would recognize me was slim to none, but I had to be cautious. No one knew who I was in this small town. I relished the anonymity of being no one, of becoming a hazy silhouette. I observed the lives of my daughters from afar. When my heart would long for them, I would take the bus to Providence, just for a day, and observe them remotely, next to the house that I knew so well. Oh, how I wanted to embrace and kiss them, but that life was foreclosed to me now. I could only hope for these brief glimpses and snapshots into their lives. From that point on, I could only live in the shadows, like a disgraced vampire who withers in the daylight.

The rest of my life is unremarkable, really. I won't bore you with the tedious details of my lonely existence. I have cherished life only by recognizing that my daughters were safe and successful. I've become a wizened lady, too old for my own good. Mallory has passed. According to the papers, Morgan has been unfortunately accused of a patient's death. She is awaiting trial for murder. Although shocked about all these recent events, I can't say it's unexpected. My life and the lives of those around me have been dramatic from the beginning. I must show myself now and emerge from that safe cocoon that I have created for myself. Morgan needs me. I need to embrace her in my arms and show her that she can latch on to my soul and body as tightly as she wants, support from a mother whom she never knew. That will soon change. Tomorrow I'm taking the bus to Norfolk, Massachusetts, to reveal myself to her as a friendly ghost from the past, come what may.

The Claw of the Magnolia was written at the beginning of the COVID-19 pandemic, and the dark nature of the book may reflect that. As can be imagined, and opposed to my other books, the writing here was a very solitary process due to this isolation. My ideas flowed while jogging alone in parks and hiking trails without a person in sight.

However, despite this solitary writing process, I'd like to extend a warm thanks to many individuals who made this book happen. First, I'd like to thank Tod Thilleman, the amazingly talented publisher at Spuyten Duvyil, who took on the task of publishing this book. He's an astute reader, writer, and creator, and I thank him immensely. My literary agent, Linda Konner, also deserves great thanks.

Dawn Raffel was the first person who read the entire manuscript and she offered insightful suggestions every step of the away. I'm grateful to her for leading me down a better path and making this novel stronger and more concise.

My previous publisher at Jaded Ibis Press, Debra Di Blasi, has always been my cheerleader, making me want to write and read better. She is a creative force who propels me on, and I'm extremely grateful to her. She is superb i every way.

A tremendous thanks to Rey Chow for her friendship and for providing me with the impetus to continue to think critically with any type of writing, whether that'd be an editorial piece or a novel. Her literary spirit is always with me.

A big thanks to David Rocklin who champions writers and directs the very innovative monthly reading series Roar Shack in Los Angeles. When my first novel was released in 2015, he invited me to his series, which was my first venture of reading to a large audience. I thank him for that opportunity and for assisting me with this novel, too.

Other people who read this book and offered invaluable comments are Jorge Armenteros, Mariam Beevi Lam, Jane Rosenberg LaForge, John Madera, and Mark Haskell Smith. I'm thankful for their wisdom and friendship.

And, last, and certainly not least, are my numerous friends and family members, especially my twin sister Pooneh, without whom none of this would be possible. There are too many people to name here, but suffice it to say, you know who you are. I extend a genuinely warm thanks to them all.

Pedram Navab is a board-certified integrative neurologist and attorney who currently resides in Los Angeles. A Fellow of the American Academy of Sleep Medicine, he has been educated at Stanford and Brown. He was nominated for a Pushcart Prize for his debut novel, *Without Anesthesia.* His second novel, *This Will Destroy You*, was a 2019 Foreword INDIES finalist. He is also the author of a non-fiction hybrid work, entitled *Sleep Reimagined.* His literary writings have been published in *Entropy*, *Big Other*, and other publications.